A TISKET A CASKET (BOOK 2)

A HARLEY AND DAVIDSON MYSTERY

LILIANA HART

LOUIS SCOTT

7TH PRESS

To the kids -
Y'all are pretty awesome, even if you eat all our food.

PROLOGUE

Orange flames danced through the attic with viciousness—devouring without prejudice—the monster growing in power as it was fed. Plumes of black smoke swirled into the night sky, and the flames hissed as powerful streams of water tried to destroy the destroyer.

Red lights flashed through the streets, a disorienting symphony of sounds and color. Everyone watched as the battle raged on, wondering who would come out the victor.

The Rio Chino Fire Department was proud of its history—a hundred and forty five years of serving the public and battling the monsters that threatened their community.

The house was old, nothing more than kindling for the flames that ate it alive. They'd been called soon enough to save some of the structure, but it was the fire department's own demons that threatened to end the tradition of brotherhood under fire.

Fire Chief Kip Grogan was a thirty-year vet with less than a year until a full and well-earned retirement. His silver shock of thinning hair and round, red cheeks made

Kip easily identifiable on any fire scene. Tonight though, he was fighting more than fire.

"Lester, get some spray on the southwest corner. It's trying to hop houses." Kip ordered over the radio.

"Trying to sir, but Gage isn't cooperating."

"Gauge, what gauge? Everything's at full pump and pressure. Pour water where I told you."

"No, it's Gage, Gage McCoy. This is his house, and he's not letting us suppress it."

"Why not?" Kip yelled over the radio and the sirens that wailed along the small suburban street.

"Said he lost it in his divorce and hopes it burns to the ground," Lester said.

"I don't care what he says," Kip said. "Arrest him."

"Except that I'm not a cop, and he is," Lester said. "And he's armed."

The roar of the hoses fighting the fire was deafening, but Kip felt the chill cross over his skin—that internal warning that told him something was about to go very, very wrong. The sound of rushing water came to a halt and there was nothing but the crackle of flames and the crash of wood as the house came down.

"What's going on?" he yelled again, but there was no answer.

He kicked open the doors of the command center truck where he'd been giving orders and was greeted with the sight of 1754 Constantine Drive fully engulfed in flames. His men stood watching. Helpless.

It didn't take long for Kip to assess the situation and understand why everything had come to a halt. A man stood, silhouetted by flame and shadow, a rifle in his hands.

He and Gage McCoy had gone through trainings together. They'd been friends. But he also knew the job changed a man. Divorce changed a man too, and Gage had gone through a doozy. But friend or no, Gage was putting lives at stake, and he was turning his back on the oath he'd promised to uphold. Well, Gage wasn't going to destroy the reputation of what he'd helped build over the last thirty years.

"Tony."

"Yes, Chief?"

"Get my gun." Kip ordered.

"The cops are on their way," Tony said.

Tony Fletcher was Kip's second in command, and he could hear the plea in his voice.

"Give it to me or get out of my command center," Kip said, challenging him. "The cops will be too late."

Kip watched as Tony reluctantly unlocked the diamond-plated metal cabin that also served as a bench seat inside the truck, and Kip held out his hand for the .45 caliber pistol, the weight familiar as he curled his fingers around the butt.

"No one is going to interfere in one of my operations," Kip said. "Not even Gage McCoy." His only thoughts were of his men, of taking out the threat before the threat took them all out.

Kip hefted his bulk out of the truck and headed for cover. He needed to be closer to make the shot. But he didn't move fast enough once his chest tightened like a vice grip. The sound of a rifle firing echoed from outside and rung in the back of the command post. Kip clutched his chest and fell face first from the back of the truck and into a puddle of backwashed water.

CHAPTER ONE

There was something about the Friday Night Lights. The smell of turf and hotdogs, the sound of an excited crowd and the cheers of the pep squad. Fall and football went hand in hand, but Hammerin' Hank Davidson wondered if Texas had gotten the memo that the temperature was supposed to be cooler in October. Since he'd moved to the Lone Star State the year before, he'd started sweating in places he didn't know it was possible to sweat.

He was still adjusting to retired life. After twenty-six years working for the Philadelphia Police Department, adjusting to civilian life hadn't been easy. He'd been trained by the FBI to do a job that most people didn't have the aptitude for, and if he was being honest, regular life was kind of...boring.

What he needed was to find something exciting to replace that life. He'd tried a few things that hadn't stuck, but he wasn't giving up yet. He hadn't met many new friends since his retirement. Being an introvert didn't make finding friends easy, but he'd taken an immediate liking to Nick Dewey.

They'd met at Cabela's while Hank was looking for a hobby to save him from his boredom. What he'd really wanted was a Harley Davidson, but he had no idea how to ride, and part of him didn't want to be the cliché of having a mid-life crisis. Fortunately, Nick had taken pity on him and introduced him to the world of hunting. He'd also introduced him to the world of high school football.

"I can't believe this stadium cost seventy-two million dollars," Hank said.

He ran his fingers through his graying hair before tugging on his ball cap, and then he leaned in closer to hear Nick's response. It was hard to combat the dueling bands and frenzied fans.

"I'd like to say Katy High School is one of a kind, but stadiums like this one aren't uncommon here in Texas. Friday night football is as much a religion to some as church is on Sundays."

Hank didn't have a dog in this particular fight. He was just along for the ride. But Nick was a Beacon City High School alum, so they'd made the trek to Katy to watch the two teams duke it out on their way to the 777 Ranch to do some hunting.

He hated to break it to Nick, but he was pretty sure hunting wasn't going to be his new retirement hobby either. He had nothing against the sport, but sitting in a deer stand for hours wasn't exactly his idea of exciting. No, he hadn't felt the rush of excitement for a good six months. Not since he'd solved a cold case with mystery writer Agatha Harley. But she'd been busy writing books, and he'd been busy trying to be retired.

Hank was in a horde of thousands, but never in his life had he ever felt so alone. He didn't want to retire. But, he knew his life depended on it. He was still at the top of his game, but time is counted differently in the world of malicious murderers and cagey cons. He smiled and hoped it would pass.

"Yikes," Nick said. "We're getting our hats handed to us this year. What do you say we head out at half? We've still got another three hours before we get to the ranch."

"Fine with me," Hank said, slightly disappointed. It was a heck of a game, and he hadn't been able to take his eyes off the Beacon City quarterback. The kid was incredible. He was a man among boys.

"Who's the QB?" he asked.

"Cole McCoy," Nick said. "Sad story, but the kid seems to have turned out okay."

"What do you mean sad?" Hank asked.

"His dad, Gage was a high school All-American football player. He ended up at SMU and played there, but wasn't good enough to make it to the pros, so he joined the police service at Rio Chino. Married his high-school sweetheart and a few years later Cole was born."

"I must be missing the sad part," Hank said.

Nick smiled, but it didn't reach his eyes. "It's a tough conversation to tell in a stadium."

"Okay, but you got me interested."

"We got a long drive. I'll tell you then."

"Deal, but I'm still not seeing the bad in being a stud QB with an All-American dad. I bet his mom is something incredible, too." Hank said.

"She was," Nick whispered. "You ready to go? It's almost the half."

Hank sighed and nodded. He really wasn't looking forward to hunting. Nick told him the only difference in hunting and police work was that one animal required a warning before shooting and the other animal required a taxidermist. The thought of killing an animal and then having it sit on his mantel for the next twenty years didn't really sit well with him.

"I'm going to hit the head on the way out," Hank told Nick. "Three hours is a long time."

Nick nodded. "I'll meet you in front of the concession stand."

Everybody seemed to have the same idea as they had and decided to leave their seats before the half ended. The crowd swelled, and Hank felt swallowed up by them. He had to breathe deeply a couple of times to keep his claustro-phobia in check, and at the same time, he was searching the crowd, looking for signs of threats. Just because he was retired didn't mean he could stop the habits of twenty six years of policing.

He looked around and found himself lost in the crowd. He couldn't see where their seats had been or where the restrooms or concessions were. It was nothing but wall-to-wall people. He was six-feet-two-inches and two-hundred and forty pounds. He should've had the advantage in any crowd. But this was Texas, and he was considered "average" in size. It's true what they said, everything *was* bigger in Texas.

"Hank!"

He stopped and looked around, and then he decided to head toward the home end zone.

"Hank!"

He stopped again, sure he heard his name this time. Who in the world would know him here other than Nick?

And that definitely wasn't Nick's voice. He scanned the crowd and finally spotted her. There was Agatha Harley, looking like a beacon in the middle of the crowd.

He didn't want to seem too eager to get to her, but he might have shoved a couple of people out of the way a little harder than necessary.

"Aggie," he said, enjoying the way her nose crinkled as soon as he called her by her nickname. "What brings you here?" He reached in to give her a hug, but it turned awkward. Neither of them knew what to do with their hands.

"My goddaughter is in the band," she said, patting him on the shoulder. "I needed a break, so figured I'd drive down to watch her perform."

She was a tall woman, around five-foot-ten, and it always amazed him she was close to forty-years old because she looked so much younger. She had that fresh-faced, girl next door look about her.

She wasn't flashy, and she wasn't the type of woman you'd do more than glance over in a crowd, but she was worth a second look. Her black hair was pulled back in a ponytail and she wasn't wearing any makeup. A dark fringe of lashes framed her bluish-green eyes, and there was a smattering of freckles across the bridge of her nose. She was wearing a pair of khaki shorts and a TCU baseball style shirt.

"Does that mean you're finished with your book?" he asked.

She'd pretty much buried herself inside her house since they'd closed the cold case they'd been working. The only time he saw her was if he happened to see her on her morning run.

All of Agatha's mysteries were based on real life cases,

and a lot of them were cold cases she'd helped solve. She was brilliant, and he'd enjoyed every second of the time they'd worked together.

"Actually, I decided not to write the book about our case."

"Are you serious?" he asked. "After everything we went through."

"When I sat down to write it, I couldn't," she said, shrugging. "It was a little too close to home. A little too personal. I knew Nicole Green. And I knew her killer. It seemed best to leave it unwritten and let it rest."

"What about your contract?" he asked.

"I've always got parts of stories and ideas written down. I just decided to pull out one of those and finish it. It's not what I wanted, but I'm satisfied with it. It's nice to finally come up for air and join the real world again."

"It's a shame we had to come to another town to see each other. I figured you'd stop by and say hi every once in a while." Hank let slip.

He hadn't meant to say that, but he'd been disappointed after they'd worked the case together that there hadn't been any other cases to work. Or that she'd seemed interested in. He understood she had to work, but it almost felt as if she'd been avoiding him for the past several months.

"I haven't even seen my own reflection in the last six months," she said, rolling her eyes and crinkling her nose. "Deadlines aren't for wimps. I get to take a short break and then I have to jump into the next one. I don't suppose you have any ideas for the plot of my next book, do you?" She grinned at him but he could see the exhaustion in the bags under her eyes.

"I might have an old case or two you could find of interest."

"Maybe you know of something more recent," she said. "Writing stories about closed cases isn't quite as exciting as the ones I can help solve."

"I can imagine," he said, raising a brow. "Once you've tasted the victory of bringing justice to victims it's hard to go back."

"I knew you'd understand." She slapped him on the shoulder. "Maybe we can get the band back together, huh?"

"I'm actually here with a friend who mentioned something about a man who could be innocent serving time over in Huntsville for killing his wife in a fire."

A light lit in Agatha's eyes and she nodded. "Must be the Gage McCoy case," she said. "There are always rumblings about his innocence. That would be perfect."

"I'll let you know," he said, eyeing the restrooms. "Good to see you, Aggie." He vaguely heard her goodbye as he made his way to the bathroom. He'd been waiting a long time.

He finally made his way back to the concessions area where he found Nick talking with a group of other men. Everyone was wearing clothes supporting the away team and looked to be in the age range of proud dads and grandads.

"Look, here's the man," Nick said, pulling Hank into the group of men.

"Sorry about that," Hank said. "This place is huge. I got lost."

"No worries," Nick said. "I was telling the guys about your career and how you seemed interested in hearing Cole McCoy's story on the drive to the ranch."

"I guess there's more to the story than I know," Hank said, shrugging.

Hank felt the flush of embarrassment creep up his neck

and face. He hated being manipulated. He gave Nick a steely stare.

An older man with the name John embroidered on his Polo shirt, grabbed Hank's hand. "Thank you for looking into this. It's long overdue."

"Well, I don't recall agreeing to look into anything, but it is certainly a tragedy."

John dropped Hank's hand.

"You and Hank are meeting us at the 777 Ranch to hunt this weekend, right Nick?" Asked John.

He looked to be late sixties, but he was leathered and weathered so it was hard to tell.

"Yessir," Nick said.

"Don't kill all of my deer," John said, looking at Hank.

"Okay," Hank said, wondering what was going on. "I'm sure it won't be a problem. It's my first time."

"You're lucky I'm letting you go at all. In fact, I'm reconsidering. I value loyalty."

"Loyalty?" Hank asked, perplexed.

John's body shook as he struggled with his thoughts. Hank knew he was operating on minimal information. His concern wasn't a hunting invitation, but not getting suckered into something he wasn't familiar with or able to do.

John pointed a crooked finger at Hank.

"You think it helps Cole for you to find the case a *tragedy*? I thought you'd agreed to help, and now you change your mind?" The man spat on the ground and Hank could tell he was getting all worked up.

"Easy now, John," Nick said. "Hank's not been briefed yet. We'll talk on the drive to the Triple Seven."

Hank was beginning to think the smartest thing he could do would be to find Agatha and catch a ride back to Rusty Gun with her.

"What the heck is going on here?" Hank asked.

"Sorry about that," Nick said, pulling him away from the group, but Hank jerked out of his grasp.

"I've spent my career reading people, Nick. But I've got to hand it to you, you had me fooled. I hate being manipulated, and I hate being backed into a corner."

Hank cut through the crowd easily—they seemed to part right in front of him—and he made his way to the parking lot. What bothered him the most was he never saw it coming. Had retirement made him lose his edge? Obviously, he and Nick meeting by chance at Cabela's hadn't really been chance at all. It had all been about the McCoy case.

Hank scrolled through his phone for Agatha's number and waited impatiently as it rang with no answer. He sent her a text message telling her not to leave without getting in touch.

"I swear, Hank, I wasn't trying to fool you," Nick said, following close behind him. "I had no idea who you were when we met. You're the one who almost hit me with that giant tent, remember? And you were the one who told me about your career. I just bragged on knowing you to the guys a little bit and things kind of took off from there."

"Well, it would've been nice to have been let in on the secret. I could've stayed home and watered my lawn. I have enough people I can't trust in my life. I didn't need to add any more." He thought of Agatha again and willed for his phone to ring. He could trust Agatha, and remembering that helped calm his temper.

"Look, I'm sorry," Nick said. "Give us a break. We're a bunch of bored millionaires, looking for something to make life exciting. You were that something. You've lived the kind of life guys like us dream about. I figured if you got interested in the case, it might benefit all."

"Far from it," Hank said. "Far from it."

Hank stopped short of the big Ford diesel pickup truck.

"Come straight with me Nick, or I'm not stepping foot in that thing. I'll walk back to Rusty Gun if I have to."

Nick reached up and dropped the tailgate. He hopped on it and invited Hank to join him.

"Look, I'm desperate, okay? Cole McCoy is my grandson. And his father was set up for murder. I know he didn't kill my Julie. Sure, they had their problems, but Gage is no murderer."

"What?" Hank asked.

"I know it sounds crazy, but it's true. And it's all because of high school football rivalry."

"You're telling me that Cole's father killed your daughter, and you want to get him out of prison?" Hank asked incredulously.

"Yes. I've made a fortune reading people, Hank. I believe him when he says he's innocent. He loved Julie. Even worse, that pack of political rats at Rio Chino would stop at nothing to frame something bad on a Beacon City alum."

"What if you're actually working to free the man who did kill your daughter?" Hank challenged him.

"I know it in my heart. I don't trust that slime ball, Tony Fletcher. He's the fire chief. I think he set up Gage to take the fall."

"You think or have proof?"

"I got my heart. And it says that boy is rotting away in Huntsville Penitentiary for a crime he didn't commit."

"Let me do some digging around before I get involved, Nick."

"Fair enough. Now, let's go hunting.

CHAPTER TWO

SATURDAY

Despite Hank's wishes, Saturday morning came earlier than he wanted. Retirement had given him a certain amount of freedom with his schedule, and he enjoyed the occasional day of sleeping past sunrise. Today would have been a great day to sleep late.

He rubbed the sleep out of his swollen eyes and thanked God for the automatic coffee machine that had it ready and waiting for him. He stumbled through the motions of putting in cream and sugar while searching for the Tylenol.

Once he'd taken the drugs, he pushed open the screen door of the hunting cabin and onto the porch, questioning his sanity as to why he thought being an outdoorsman and retirement should go hand in hand. He was fifty-two years old and had never been an outdoorsman, so why did he think it would be a good hobby? Because he was an idiot, that's why.

"Stupid idea. I'm waiting to kill animals, but instead they're watching and waiting to kill me." He took a sip and waited for the jolt to hit his senses. "I can feel your eyes on me," he said loudly, and his head jerked to the side as something rustled in the brush.

The morning sky was painted with streaks of pink and orange over pale blue. Dew covered the scorched and cracked earth but it wouldn't last long before the sun burned it off. Hank had spent some time in Texas during the course of his career, and he and his wife had taken a memorable weekend to San Antonio years before, but he'd never taken the time to realize how vast and different it was.

Since Agatha had been busy with her book, and his friend Reggie Coil had been busy being sheriff, that had left Hank with a lot of free time on his hands. He'd taken to packing a couple of sandwiches and a thermos of coffee and driving to all parts of the state. And he'd come to realize in the short time he'd been there that Texas was like a whole other country.

The ranch in Hondo was more than he expected, but he should've guessed a millionaire's idea of roughing it would be quite a bit different than his own. It was a two-story log cabin structure with every convenience known to man, including a cook and a housekeeper. He expected the hunting experience to be equally convenient. Maybe the deer laid down first to make it easy to kill them.

He shook his head at the ridiculousness of it all. This was definitely not him. But he was here, so he might as well make the best of it. The ranch hands had obviously been busy. The all-terrain transport buggies were being loaded with weapons and ice chests.

Hank went back to his room to deck himself out in full-fledged south Texas desert-patterned camouflage. He hadn't spoken to Nick since their exchange in the parking lot the night before. It had been a long three-hour drive to the ranch. But when Hank went back into the kitchen to refill his coffee, Nick was there.

Nick looked at him sheepishly. "I'm sorry again about last night. Can we put it behind us and focus on bagging some bucks?"

"Sure," Hank said. "We might as well make the best of it."

"How about you get the first trophy buck we see?" Nick pointed to a massive deer head mounted proudly in the main common area.

Hank laughed and shook his head, wondering how Nick could have spent any time with him at all and not known what he would and wouldn't do. "Charity is something I won't accept. I'll bag my own."

"Understood, but I'll make sure the boys walk one close enough to where you can pet it before you shoot it," Nick said, laughing.

"Well, maybe in that case, I'll take the shot. It is my first time, after all." Hank grinned and felt the tension ease from his shoulders.

"I already feel like a traitor for telling the guys who you were. If you don't want to do this just say the word and I'll have a chopper get you back to Rusty Gun. They're good men, but once they get something in their head it's hard to change their mind."

Hank wasn't used to discussing feelings, and he wasn't used to hanging out with men who weren't cops. It was weird. What did he and a bunch of millionaires have in common anyway?

"Hey, Nick."

"Yeah, Hank?"

"I'm really sorry about Julie."

"I appreciate you saying that."

Hank followed Nick back outside and they got the thumbs up from the ranch hands that they were good to go. Dawn hadn't quite surrendered to morning as they got in one of the buggies.

Two hours later, Hank wished he'd taken Nick up on the helicopter ride back to Rusty Gun. The deer hunting stand was an open platform structure with an elevation of about twenty-one feet to allow for an expansive view of his target areas. He hadn't seen a deer all morning.

The quiet had given him too much time to think. Staying busy was how he kept the memories of his job at bay—memories of his wife. His mind raced with images of the victims. He never forgot them. Or those who'd murdered them. He'd slapped the handcuffs on hundreds of violent killers in his career.

He soon discovered that without some sort of distraction or stimulation that his mind roamed back to where it was most comfortable, and most tortured. It was why he'd retired when he did. Twenty-six-years of corpses stacked up quickly until Hank couldn't see anything but their faces.

He checked his phone again, happy to see that the spotty service had him connected to the outside world, though he knew it was brief. It had been on and off all morning. It vibrated in his hand as it updated. He had two messages and three text messages from Agatha. He read the text messages first.

Started looking into the McCoy case. You picked a winner.

"Thank God," he whispered. Even the thought of giving into Nick's friends didn't deter him. He had to get the heck out of here. And the thought of working with Agatha again cheered him right up. He scrolled to the next text.

Nick and Gage McCoy are connected. Be careful.

I was told. Could be a sad story, or a misguided effort.

Hank couldn't stop thinking about how Nick had led him into taking this case. Would it be too much to ask of a friend? After all, Hank had used Nick to learn about hunting. Did that make him untrustworthy? It was all so much more than a fun weekend of hunting. Now Hank was questioning his own motives.

He shoved the cell phone into his vest pocket and grabbed the red assistance alert button Nick had given him when Nick had dropped him at the stand. Nick had told him the device was to be used in the event of an injury or downed deer. Hank didn't care about the rules. He was ready to get out of this charade.

His cell phone buzzed again, and it was from a number he didn't recognize. But the message made it clear it was probably one of the ranch hands.

Forty-five minutes.

"Freaking great," Hank said. "Glad it's not too big of an emergency."

Hank rolled over onto his back, weaved fingers behind his head, and closed his eyes. He might as well get a nap in while he waited. But his last thought before he drifted off was that he would look into the Gage McCoy case, but it had nothing to do with Nick and his manipulations. If there was the slightest chance an innocent man was in prison, then he owed it to that boy throwing all the touchdown passes to give him his father back.

But if the man was guilty...he could rot.

CHAPTER THREE

SUNDAY

"Wow, this place is a mess."

Agatha stood and surveyed her office with a critical eye. She'd been in work mode the past few months, and she'd had to work harder and longer hours than usual because she'd had to start the latest book from scratch. Her only focus had been the book. She'd rarely left the house—only for the occasional lunch with Heather or a trip to the grocery store to replenish her T.V. dinners.

The housekeeper had come in once a week to make sure laundry was done and the sheets were changed, and she kept the rest of the house vacuumed and dusted. But she was under strict orders never to touch the office while Agatha was working. She was going to have to give the poor woman a raise.

Agatha rolled up her sleeves and got busy picking up trash and empty cups. Books were scattered everywhere and an inch of dust covered her desk and the table she used for research. She needed a clean slate. A fresh start. Because she had a new project. And she also didn't want Hank to see how she'd been living. He seemed like the spit and polish type to her, and he wouldn't appreciate the disorder of creativity.

She was glad she'd gone to the game over the weekend. The McCoy case was one that had interested her for the last decade, but the case had involved a cop and a firefighter, and she wasn't part of the club. Meaning cops and firefighters were territorial about their own, and they didn't talk out of school, even if one of them was guilty. But now she had Hank to get her in.

Once the office was clean, she went and showered and put on a pair of tattered gray sweats and an old TCU shirt that was threadbare in places. She put her hair up in a messy bun on top of her head and considered herself ready to get down to business. One of the greatest things about working from home was that she could wear pants with an elastic waistband every day.

Agatha went back to her office and assembled every piece of information she could find on the McCoy case. She gathered Rio Chino maps and stacked them on the end of her conference table, and she searched for every newspaper article and social media post she could find.

There was a thud against her front door, and she perked up at the thought of the Sunday newspaper waiting on her front porch.

She opened her front door, stuck her head out and looked from side to side, grabbed her paper, and then closed the door again. The *Rusty Gun Gazette* wasn't more than a dozen or so pages thick, but it was the best way to keep abreast of the latest happenings.

Like always, she flipped to the Obituaries section. Some of her best book ideas came from reading about the lives of other people. But she froze as she saw the name of Walter

Green. She and Hank had finally given Walter's daughter, Nicole, the peace she deserved a few months back by discovering her killer.

Everyone thought Walter had been the one to kill his daughter, and while it was true he'd been a horrible person in general, he didn't kill Nicole. And now the whole family was buried in the Rusty Gun Cemetery. Just like that, an entire lineage was wiped out.

Agatha thought often about her legacy. Maybe because she was an only child and her parents had died relatively young. All she had was work. She had no family. No children to leave an inheritance to. She was thirty-eight years old, and marriage had never been on her radar. Much less children. She guessed she was past that stage in her life. Her career had been her complete focus, especially after her parents had died.

Who did she have that she could leave a legacy for? Her goddaughter would inherit everything, but she didn't know the real Agatha. Who would be left to tell stories of the kind of woman she'd been. It was a depressing thought. She thought of her mother, and wished she'd spent more time talking to her about the Harley family. All she knew were her grandparents names and that she had visited them on occasion.

Agatha exhaled deeply as she allowed her eyes to stare until they crossed at the Sunday paper. She tried to conjure up a faded memory of her dad at the same table. He loved the paper after church. As a child, she would sit in his lap and try to read the words. Maybe it was something in the air that had her missing her mom and dad.

There was another thud against the front door and she shook herself out of the gloom that had suddenly come over her.

"Hank," she whispered, and launched herself up from the table.

It had been good to see him at the game. Maybe too good. She'd missed his company. When she had managed to drag herself away from her book the past months, he'd always seemed to be gone. She'd knocked on his door a couple of times to see if he wanted to grab lunch, but she guessed retirement was keeping him busy. She hadn't swallowed her pride and allowed herself to text or call him, thinking maybe she'd hear from him first. But she hadn't.

She wondered how Hank felt about being fifty-two-years-old without family. Maybe he had the same thoughts she did about legacies. She'd have to ask him. But then she had the thought that maybe he did have children. They'd never talked about it.

She'd asked him once whether he'd ever been married, but he'd shut that conversation down quickly. She could read between the lines well enough to know that he probably had been at some point, but it hadn't ended well. Maybe he'd had children from that union. The thought intrigued her. It reminded her how little she really knew about Hank Davidson.

Another knock on the door shook her from her thoughts.

"Well, hello Hank. Funny seeing you here." She said.

"You invited me." He frowned.

"And that I did. Why are you just standing there?"

"Because you've not moved to let me in. I'm guessing I'm still invited." He said.

"Yes, I guess so." She teased.

Agatha stepped to the side of the threshold. Hank was a big man, a couple of inches over six feet, and his shoulders and chest were broad. As her friend Heather liked to say, he was *all man*. Agatha would've been dead not to notice. And boy, had she noticed.

He was dressed in jeans and a gray Philadelphia PD t-shirt, and she was happy to see he'd retired the Birkenstocks for a pair of tennis shoes. He'd cropped his hair shorter, probably out of convenience more than style, but she could still see the smattering of gray throughout the dark strands. His face was angular, his cheeks freshly shaved, and the lines around his eyes and mouth made him look comfortable in his age. His eyes were dark brown, and his shoulders... well, she'd had a lot of time to think about his shoulders. They were really good shoulders.

"Hello? Agatha?" Hank asked.

Heat flushed her cheeks when she realized he'd been trying to get her attention. "Hey, neighbor. I'm sorry for being so distracted."

Then she looked at him a little closer. He was kind of green.

"You feeling okay? You don't look so good."

"I feel much better than I did," he said, heading straight back to her "war room," as he liked to call her office. "I think I can officially say that Nick and I are no longer hunting buddies. When I requested the chopper to take me home early, I think he paid the pilot to give me an experience, if you get my meaning. It wasn't a smooth trip. I pretty much face planted in the bed last night and didn't move until this morning. The room is still spinning a bit."

He looked over the room, familiarizing himself with it, and then went to the kitchen to make himself a cup of coffee. At least he still felt comfortable in her home.

"So are you going to tell me what's up?" he asked.

"What do you mean?" her voice pitched up.

"I mean, you look upset about something."

"We've barely seen each other in six months, and you think you can tell when I'm upset about something?" she asked, raising an eyebrow.

"Yep," he said, grinning. "When partners work together you get to know a lot about a person by their facial expressions and body language. Just for future reference, you should never play poker." He warned.

"Good to know," she said. Then she went over to the chaise and grabbed the paper, and then she laid it on the conference table. "Walter Green is dead."

"Ahh," he said. And there seemed to be a complete world of understanding in that one word. "Things like this bring life into perspective. It reminds us of our own mortality."

She let out a whoosh of breath and fell back in the chair. He did understand.

"Hey, I got you something," he said, picking up a wrapped package from the floor. He'd obviously set it down while he'd been making coffee, and she'd completely missed it. No wonder he'd realized something was off. She normally noticed everything.

"Oh, wow," she said. "I don't know what the special occasion is, but I love it."

"You haven't even opened it."

"I don't care," she said, feeling a little misty-eyed. "I couldn't tell you the last time someone got me a gift."

"Not even for your birthday?" Hank asked, shocked.

"Maybe so, and I think it was my mom who gave it." Her thoughts drifted back to sentimental.

"It must've meant so much."

"I think people look at me as this eccentric woman who has a lot of money, but they're not really sure what I do or how I earn it. And I love buying gifts for others or donating to little league and stuff like that. Giving is one of my favorite things to do with what I've been blessed with. But people don't get me gifts because they think if I want something, I'll just buy it myself. But I love getting them, no matter what it is. It means someone is thinking about you, and that means a lot."

"I guess I never looked at it that way. But I'm glad I was able to bring that smile to your face. I might start giving you stuff every day." Hank laughed.

Agatha chuckled, a feeling of warmth spreading through her, and she ripped into the paper to reveal a white box. When she lifted the lid she gasped.

"It's not much, but I thought it was fun."

"Are you kidding me? It's awesome."

Inside was a wooden sign with carved letters. It read:

A.C. Riddle's War Room
Justice in Progress

TEARS FELL before she could control them. She'd meant it when she'd told him she couldn't remember the last gift she'd gotten. But she'd remember his thoughtfulness forever.

"Hey, kid," Hank said, looking a little panicked. "Don't cry. I'm not good with crying."

"Me either," she said, sniffling. "Sorry. I'm going to hang it right there on the wall, where I can always see it."

Hey Aggie," Hank's voice quieted. "I really am sorry for the loss of your parents. Mine died when I was very young. You never get over it, so please don't feel like you should apologize for crying over them."

"Do you still cry, Hank?"

"I grieve because I don't remember them except through photos. But, I miss them dearly."

Agatha sniffled and wiped her face. A slight smile appeared as her hands parted.

"Okay, I'm fine. Let's focus on McCoy."

"Great," he said. "What do you say we get to work?"

"I feel like there are important details you're leaving out," she said when he reached for his keys and jangled them in front of her.

"Coil wants to meet with us," he said. "And no, before you ask, I don't know why. But you look like you could get out of the house for a little while. You're very pale. Did you see any sun this summer?"

"I told you, I was working. And I got out Friday night to go to the game."

"You're a real party animal, Agatha Harley." She grabbed her purse and followed him out the door. She locked it behind her. "Besides, I'm not that pale."

"Honey, you're so pale I can see through your skin."

"Don't call me honey."

"You got it, Aggie."

CHAPTER FOUR

RUSTY GUN, TEXAS WASN'T A BIG TOWN—JUST OVER eighteen hundred people—but it was a close-knit community of multi-generational families who'd worked, bled, and supported one another for almost two hundred years. Unless you were a Beauregard or a Hatchett. If you were unfortunate enough to have either of those surnames there'd been nothing but two hundred years of feuding.

The town didn't scrimp on the holidays, and Halloween was no exception. The buildings on Main Street had been lined with orange lights, and the front windows of every business had been painted with a unique Halloween scene. Witches and goblins and ghouls decorated front yards and lamp posts.

"I love this time of year," Agatha said. "On Halloween all the businesses stay open late and hand out candy. The café sells Witches' Brew and puts things on the menu like Spaghetti and Eyeballs. They've been doing it that way since long before I was born. When I was little my parents would bring me down here in my costume, and then we'd stop by the café for a treat when I was finished. They were always good memories."

"Interesting," Hank said. "In my experience, Halloween is when all the crazies come out and it's best to go on shift with an extra set of cuffs and a cross around your neck."

"That does sound like a different experience," Agatha said, lips twitching.

It had taken almost ten minutes to drive from Agatha's house to Main Street, but they found a parking spot right in front of the Bell County Sheriff's Office. It didn't help that it was right next to the empty parking spot that had belonged to Kim Lee, Sheriff Coil's former secretary. She was currently serving time for the role she played when her son killed Nicole Green. The sheriff's secretary job hadn't been filled yet.

"Why do you think he wants to see us?" Agatha asked, both nervous and excited. They were still in the Jeep, but Hank had already unbuckled and had his hand on the door handle.

"I told you I didn't know," Hank said. "You'll find out soon enough if you'll get out of the car and stop asking me questions."

"Touchy," Agatha said under her breath but did as he said and got out of the car. "You and Coil hung out any since the arrests were made?"

Hank scowled at her. "Not really. He's a little busy now that he's having to be the sheriff and secretary."

She could see the guilt in Hank's eyes, and knew it was no use telling him it wasn't his fault. Kim Lee had made her own choices. And they'd been the wrong ones. The consequences were hers to bear.

Agatha raised her brows when she walked in. The whole office was being renovated. It was amazing how much bigger it looked now that the wood-paneling and shag carpeting was gone.

Coil stood across the room with the contractor, his arms crossed over his chest. He wore his typical uniform—a plaid button-down shirt with his sheriff's star pinned over the pocket, a pair of worn jeans, boots, and a Stetson.

Coil waved them over. "You guys are here early. I figured I'd have to go to church service and get back before you got here."

"You want us to come back later?" Hank asked.

"Nah, we can go to the late service. We never go to that service because it's too hard to beat the Baptists to lunch, but this time will be fine. I had to come into the office anyway to let Larry in. He's agreed to work on Sundays so there's not so much chaos during the work week. But it's coming along nicely. Should be done with the interior stuff by the end of next week."

"It's definitely improved, even with the sheet rocked walls and the concrete floors," Hank said.

"Y'all come on back to the office with me and we'll let Larry work in peace."

Agatha followed behind Hank and Coil and wondered if she was reading more into the tension between Hank and Coil than she should have. Something just felt off.

Agatha took the chair in front of Coil's desk, but Hank remained standing. So did Coil.

"I've been doing a lot of thinking about the Nicole Green case," Coil said. "It was my fault for it not being able to be solved eight years ago. I take responsibility for that. But the fact of the matter is, even with my screw up, I took a big chance at handing that file over to you. We got lucky because Tyler pleaded guilty to avoid the death penalty, but we could've gotten our hats handed to us if we'd been questioned over how certain information was gained. We didn't exactly follow procedure, even though we got the results we wanted."

"What are you saying?" Agatha asked.

"What I am suggesting is that we make things a little more official. Just in case we ever need to cover our butts."

"I've known you a long time, Reg," Hank said. "I know I'm going to hate whatever you suggest, so you might as well spit it out."

Coil grinned, a dimple showed in his right cheek. "Well then, as long as you know you're going to hate it, how about we make things more official?"

"Nope," Hank said. "I'm not going back."

It was obvious to Agatha he'd been expecting Coil to say that. Hank had never told her why he'd retired, but there'd obviously been a reason. His face had paled and she could see the anxiety in his eyes. She wanted to get up and hug him, but she knew he'd just push her away.

"Take it easy, pal," Coil said, holding up both hands. "You're retired, and no one will change that decision except for you. I promise. All I'm suggesting it that you carry this badge. For official reasons."

Coil tossed a polished, six-point deputy Sheriff's star set in a leather wallet onto his desk. The Texas state seal caught Agatha's eye, and then she read the blue embossed letters that circled the seal: *Bell County Special Investigator.*

"What's this about?" Hank asked, eyeing the star as if it were a poisonous snake.

"There's no obligation, other than to list you as a reserve commission deputy. This will cover all of our butts in the event something comes up, or pieces of information are learned by you that might lead to an arrest or prosecution."

Hank's eyes never left the badge, but he didn't move to

pick it up. "I carried one badge for twenty-six years. It feels strange to start carrying another."

"Right now you're just a nosy civilian. And nosy civilian's end up getting sued or shot. You've got your weapon, and you're authorized to help and use it if the need arises. But this makes the paperwork easier on all sides."

"Will it get us out of speeding tickets?" Agatha asked.

Coil's lips twitched. "Yes."

"We'll take it," she said, snatching it off the desk.

"Slow down, tiger," Hank said. "There has to be a catch. There's always a catch."

Agatha looked at Coil expectantly and raised her brows.

"It's for both of our protection," Coil said. "But yes, there's a little catch."

"Told ya," Hank said.

"All I ask is that y'all look through this stack of old case files. Larry found it in a closet that had been plastered over decades ago. I thumbed through, and I gotta tell ya, there's some juicy stuff in those boxes."

"How juicy?" Agatha asked

"Book writing juicy." And then Coil looked at Hank. "And boredom-curing juicy."

"Fine," Hank said. "But if I don't feel comfortable with it after a while I'm giving it back."

"You're sure this'll get us out of speeding tickets?" Agatha asked.

"Him, yes," Coil said, grinning. "You, no."

Hank snatched the badge out of her hand. "I'll take that," he said, and put the wallet in his back pocket.

"There's always a catch," Agatha said.

CHAPTER FIVE

HANK INSISTED THEY SWITCH CARS FOR THE LONG drive to Rio Chino. Not that he minded Agatha driving. It's just that he preferred to do it. He didn't like giving up control.

"Why are we going to Rio Chino?" Hank asked. "The only thing I know about this case is that a guy set his house on fire and murdered his wife, and everyone thinks he's innocent."

"Not everyone," Agatha said. "There were plenty of people to say they weren't surprised. As far as divorces go, this one was *TMZ* worthy."

"The level of interest just doesn't make sense. I get accosted by a group of rich guys, thinking I'm their savior and going to look into a case that's been closed for ten years. I tell them I haven't even heard of the case, and they treat me like I've just stolen the silver. Then they take me to this dude ranch, ignore me, and then try to kill me on the helicopter ride back. And for what? A house fire and a high school QB? It's nuts."

"It's a hunting ranch. Not a dude ranch," Agatha said, correcting him.

"Whatever. I'd still like to know the big deal."

Agatha scrunched up in the BMW's leather seat and exhaled as she reluctantly tugged out a few briefing sheets she'd printed earlier.

"Back in 2008, the Rio Chino Fire Department responded to a residential fire. Apparently, its point of origin was pretty much everywhere, and the place went up like a tinderbox. Firefighters followed standard procedure and put water on the blaze, but Gage McCoy stood out front with a shotgun and refused to let them put out the fire. He lost it in the divorce and said he'd rather see it burned to the ground.

"Once the fire was extinguished, Gage was arrested. And when the embers cooled enough to go through what was left of the place, they found the body of his ex-wife, Julie McCoy. She'd been handcuffed to the bed. There wasn't much left of her, but the medical examiner found a bullet in her chest."

"Thank God for small favors," Hank said.

"Why's that?" Agatha asked.

"Because a bullet in the chest is a heck of a lot better way to die than burning to death."

Agatha cringed. "Good point. The fire chief also died that night."

Hank changed lanes and tapped the brakes, annoyed by the amount of traffic. "What? McCoy killed the fire chief?"

"No. Kip Grogan was his name. He had a heart attack, but that went a long way in convincing a jury to convict McCoy."

"So, big picture, what are we up against? What's the town's climate toward Gage, post-conviction relief efforts, forensic reevaluations? Really, anything to get a foothold and get a leg up on this case. Because Nick swears Gage is innocent."

"It comes down to it being a town rivalry," Agatha said. "Gage McCoy is a hero in the city of Beacon City, loved by everyone. But because the incident took place in Rio Chino, there's still the chill thanks to poor old Kip dropping dead. Gage reached out through a prison ministry to the Innocence Project, but politics put a stop to that before it could start and they didn't take his case. Everything I got from public records requests show the evidence that wasn't washed away from the fire hoses still sits at the RCPD."

"A lot of good that's going to do us."

"Why don't you call your friend Nick and see what he can do to help us?" Agatha suggested. "Money paves the way for a lot of information."

"You think he's going to be agreeable to bribing law enforcement officials?"

"I think he'll do whatever is necessary to see his daughter's killer brought to justice."

Hank took the Rio Chino exit, and it wasn't long before they passed the city limits. According to the sign, a little more than twenty-thousand people called Rio Chino home. Downtown had that small-town feel, even though it was a good sized town—old brick buildings and a gothic courthouse in the square.

"Geez," Hank said. "What's with all the football decorations? Don't they know it's Halloween? There's not a witch in sight. Not even any cobwebs. You wouldn't know it was Halloween this week. What's the deal with these football rivalries?

Agatha sighed and said, "Your Yankee is showing. This is Texas. Football means everything. Cities shut down for it.

People lose their paychecks over it. And rivalries are instilled from the cradle. Every town has a rivalry that's the highlight of the season. It just so happens Rio Chino and Beacon City have that special bond."

Hank sat at the red light, but he didn't move once the light turned green.

"I get being a football fan. I've been a Philadelphia Eagles fan my whole life."

"Yeah, I wouldn't admit that to anyone in Cowboy country," Agatha said.

"But that doesn't mean I would decorate my pickup truck, my high school, my storefront, or my body with team colors. I just don't understand how high school football could be so much bigger here than the rest of the country?"

"Haven't you ever seen the movie *Friday Night Lights*? Texas football is all people eat and breathe for 10 weeks out of the year. And at the end of this week, it'll be decided which team takes home the Iron Pumpkin. Rio Chino and Beacon City have been passing that pumpkin back and forth since 1946. This game is always the week of Halloween. It's a classic game of rich versus poor. David and Goliath."

Hank shook his head, amused at her enthusiasm. "Maybe one day I'll come to understand spending seventy million dollars on a high school football stadium. My old school back in Philly had a set of aluminum bleachers and a cinder block concession stand. Band parents used to work the concessions so their kids could play the tuba. This is all new to me."

"Welcome to Texas, my friend."

Hank checked the GPS and turned on his blinker, making a right and then a left off of Main Street. And then they were in front of the last place Gage McCoy had been employed. The Rio Chino Police Department.

"Do you really think we'll make any progress here?" Agatha asked. "I'm not one to be dramatic, but I have a really bad feeling about this."

Hanks's eyes scanned the outside of the justice complex. It was a two-story brick building. No frills or fuss. There was visitor parking in the front, and a ten-foot chain-link fence with an electronic gate where the cops parked their units and entered into the building from the backside.

"Is this a cop or fire town?" Hank asked.

"Is there such a thing?"

"Absolutely. It's politics. Two alpha groups are vying for the public's support and approval. Think about it. Boston is a fire town, where New York is all about its cops. So, what kind of town this?"

He watched Agatha give the police department a good look before craning her head around to see the fire department on the opposite corner.

"Yeah, wow, I get your point. Definitely a fire town."

A brand new building sat catty-corner from the police station. The smooth sandstone and modern design made it stick out like a sore thumb from the rest of the old architecture in the city. It was an ostentatious display of glass, stainless steel, and stone. And in front of the structure was an enormous bronze statue of a man decked out in his fire gear.

"I'm guessing that's the departed fire chief," Agatha said, pointing to the statue.

"Let's start at the PD. You know they'll have nothing good to say about their neighbors."

"Isn't it funny how the two cultures clash?" Agatha asked more as a rhetorical question.

"Always have. Always will. But, I know it was hard for

the police department to investigate their very own. No matter the crime, it always is."

"The PD didn't investigate McCoy," Agatha said. "The Fire Investigator did."

They got out of the car and headed up the stairs to the police lobby, but Hank stopped just outside the glass double doors, his brows raised.

"You mean to tell me that the police department didn't conduct this investigation?" Hank let go of the door and went back down the stairs. "Change of plans. Let's pay homage to old Kip."

"Think it's a better start?" Agatha asked, following him across the street.

"I'm not sure, but being they were the ones that made the arrest based on the fire investigator's findings, I don't know how we can start anywhere else."

"From everything I can tell, the fire department justified taking the lead because they said they were the victims. They were pretty ticked their streak of putting out fires was put to an end when Gage prevented them from extinguishing the fire and it burned to the ground. They even went to the district attorney to make sure they had investigative authority."

"Where in this civilized world would a victim actually get to do their own investigation?" Hank asked. "Did this case go to a jury trial or was a plea deal offered to avoid the death penalty?"

"I remember the trial and all the news reports. Everything splashed across the news was about the death of the fire chief, and how Gage's actions were what caused Kip's heart attack. There was barely any mention of Julie McCoy. Nothing about how she'd been handcuffed to the bed. If you wanted to find out the details you had to look at the transcripts. Gage ended up taking a plea deal for life in prison to avoid the death penalty. His attorney advised him not to make any statements to the media, but Gage has insisted all along that he's innocent."

"I think I'm starting to see where this is heading," Hank said.

"You know who did it?" she asked

"No, but I'm starting to think maybe Nick is right about opening this thing back up. Something smells rotten. Let's find out what it is."

CHAPTER SIX

The Rio Chino Station House One was freaking incredible. Hank had been in plenty of public safety facilities across America, but this was by far the most advanced. And it seemed totally out of place in a town the size of Rio Chino. He could only imagine what the bond looked like that had to pass to build it.

The front of the station was an open area, and then to the right were three bays that held fire trucks and an ambulance. Educational literature was neatly displayed at the help desk, and giant portraits of their most esteemed fire chiefs hung on the wall behind it. There were framed black and white pictures denoting the fire department's history all around the room. It was an impressive sight.

"Hey there," a middle-aged woman with short blonde hair said. "I'm Carla. How can I help y'all today?" She was decked out in the red and yellow of the football team. There was a team calendar on the wall and red and yellow pompoms hanging from the corners of the help desk.

"Wow," Agatha said. "Go Tigers."

Carla smiled and said, "I spotted y'all as out-of-towners

right away. Most everyone is still in church services, but even their Sunday best is red and yellow. This is an important week. Most of the businesses in town will be closed up Thursday and Friday in preparation for the big game."

"I hear Beacon City is tough this year," Hank said.

Carla's smile vanished, and she stared at him like he had three heads and none of them were attractive.

"He's from Philadelphia," Agatha said, jumping in quickly. "He doesn't understand."

Carla's look of scorn turned to one of pity as she stared him up and down. "You'll get used to it. So, what can I do for y'all?"

"We're actually here to cover the game," Hank said, coming up with the lie easily. "It's the ten-year anniversary since Gage McCoy made national news after killing his wife and being culpable for the death of the fire chief at the time. Since he's a Beacon City hero and he was a police officer her in Rio Chino, it's a good time to remind the public about what happened when we report on the game."

Carla's friendly smile disappeared. "We don't talk about that here. The past is the past."

"We think it's a great time to bring recognition to Kip Grogan," Agatha said. "I see y'all have him memorialized in front of the station. Don't you think the people would like to see that?"

"Is there anything else I can help you with?" Carla said, brow raised in defiance.

"There sure is," Hank said, smiling. It was the smile he gave criminals right before he was about to interrogate them. Carla's smirk turned into a look of concern and she took a step back. "You can get us your supervisor or someone who is qualified to answer our questions since this is going on public record. I'd hate for it to seem like the fire department has something to hide."

Carla stared at him a few seconds as if she wanted to argue, but she nodded curtly and turned on her heel to go into the back.

"You think she's coming back?" Agatha asked.

"No, but someone will. Whoever's been watching us on camera. Don't look up," he said, anticipating her next move.

"Wowza," Agatha said as a man came out the same door Carla had entered.

Hank found himself annoyed at Agatha's reaction. But even he had to admit the guy was impressive. The man had an inch or two on Hank in height and his body was all muscle. The sleeves of his shirt barely fit around his biceps and his dark blue tactical pants fit around a trim waist. His hair was cut close to the scalp in a buzz, but it was light in color. His eyes were a piercing blue.

"Welcome to Rio Chino," he said, stretching out a hand. "I'm Chief Fletcher, but you can call me Tony."

It didn't go past Hank's notice that the man was only making eye contact with Agatha, as if he weren't even there.

Agatha held out her hand to shake his and smiled. "Hi, Chief Tony."

Their hands lingered a little too long in Hank's opinion and he cleared his throat.

"Is there something I can help you with? Carla says you're here for the big game."

"That's right," Agatha said. "I can't wait to cheer on the..."

"Tigers," Tony said when Agatha couldn't come up with the name.

"Right, the Tigers."

Enough was enough in Hank's mind. Clearly Agatha's

brain was a mush pile of hormones because all she'd done was smile since the man walked into the room. Sure, the guy looked like Hercules, but her reaction was a little over the top in his opinion. Tony was spending a little too much time looking at Agatha too. He recognized that look in the other man's eyes and his protective instincts came into play.

"We do plan on covering the big game for our story," Hank said. "But it's also the ten-year anniversary of your old fire chief's death and the arrest of Gage McCoy. Our boss wants us to include the history of the Iron Pumpkin game—the good, the bad, and the ugly."

Hank waited to see how Tony would respond. It would tell him a lot about what he was up against. But Tony just smiled, though it didn't reach his eyes. He was good at playing the part of politician.

"Sir, I'd love to help you," he said. "But I'm super busy getting our equipment back in operational shape. We had a doozy three-alarmer last night, and the trucks have to be rehabilitated." Tony wiped a bit of smudge off of his nose. "We're all on twenty-four hour shifts, so we have a limited amount of time before the next shift comes on."

"Looks like you got a full crew in there to me, Chief. Don't you think you could spare a few minutes to give us a quote?" Agatha asked. She gave him a flirtatious smile ."We'll give you and the department full credit."

Tony moved in a little closer to Agatha and Hank narrowed his eyes.

"Where y'all from?" Tony asked.

"Philadelphia," Hank said.

"Wow, that's a long way. I knew the Iron Pumpkin was popular, but I didn't realize it was getting national attention. You think it'll get some ESPN coverage?"

"I think you can count on it," Hank said.

"I can carve out a few minutes for you," Tony said, leading them to a sitting area.

Agatha took a seat on the couch and Tony sat close to her, in the middle, so Hank had no choice but to take the chair facing them. He didn't like how Tony had moved in so easily, putting his arm on the back of the couch casually as if he and Agatha were sitting there "together."

Hank pulled out a notebook from his pocket and a pen and opened it up. "Like I said, we want the good, the bad and the ugly about the rivalry between Rio Chino and Beacon City. There's been plenty of dirty antics and tricks between the teams and communities over the years, but nothing brought attention to these two towns like what happened ten years ago. How long have you lived here?"

"My whole life," Tony said. "Born and raised here. Played high school ball. Opted out of college to go to the fire academy. I've been doing that ever since. Became chief when Kip died."

"Tell me about Gage McCoy."

Tony's eyes opened wide.

"Gage and I are the same age. Played against each other in high school." Tony shrugged, but there was something in the way he said it that made Hank think there was something more there. "Then he married Julie Dewey. We went to school together, so after they got married they decided to live here in Rio Chino. It wasn't easy for Gage, I'll give him that. People have long memories here, and Gage was the starting quarterback for the Beacon City team that won them the Iron Pumpkin four years in a row. He joined Rio Chino PD, and he and Julie made it work for a few years. They had a kid, and word is he'll be starting quarterback against us this Friday night."

"I've seen him play," Hank said, just to rub him the

wrong way. "He's incredible. You guys are in for a challenge."

Tony chuckled. "It'll be an even match. We have the number one defense in the nation."

"What happened with McCoy?"

Tony shrugged. "Who knows. Maybe the job started to get to him. It does all of us to some degree. But he and Julie started having problems and then everything went downhill from there. He went nuts. And the rest is public record."

"The fire department investigate Julie's murder?" Agatha asked.

"The fire marshal did," Tony said. "McCoy was arrested for interfering in the official duties of firefighters, aggravated arson, and first degree murder. He was also charged for contributing to the death of Kip Grogan, but those charges were eventually dropped. He took a plea deal and ended up with life."

"You know, you can tell a lot about people by the way they answer questions," Hank said.

"How's that?" Tony asked.

"Did you notice how you prioritized the offenses? You listed the offense against your agency before the taking of a life. And how in the world can a person be charged for someone else having a heart attack? That's the most ridiculous thing I've ever heard."

"Then it sounds like to me you should be talking to the fire marshal," Tony said, standing up. "Gage McCoy got what he had coming to him. He never belonged here, and all it got him was trouble."

"Where can we find the fire marshal?"

"Peter Chaffe? He's probably over at the high school. They've got a big assembly this afternoon to kick off Iron Pumpkin week. The whole town will practically be there.

They put the overflow in the stadium and they watch it all on the big screen. Lots of people bring picnics and stuff. It's a real family event."

"Thanks for your time," Hank said.

"I never asked your name," Tony said, looking at Agatha.

"It's Agatha," she said. "We appreciate you talking to us."

"Maybe if you're around this week we could grab a bite to eat. I'm off the next two days."

"Oh," Agatha said.

"She'll have to get back to you," Hank said. "We've got a story to write." He looked at Agatha expectantly and she seemed to come to her senses.

"Right," she said. And then she looked back at Tony. "Dinner sounds good. Let me check my schedule."

CHAPTER SEVEN

THE FIRE DEPARTMENT'S BUILDING WAS WAY BEYOND the town's financial means or tax base's capacity to borrow money against bonds. Even the police department, which was nowhere near on the same scale, looked to have cost more than the agricultural and cattle town could afford.

They'd seen enough of the town on their way in to get a feel for the area and community. It wasn't a wealthy area. Far from it. They got back in the car, and Hank turned over the ignition.

"Why would they build monuments when most folks live in shacks?" Hank asked. "And how did the bonds pass to build some of these structures when it looks like people are barely scraping by?"

"Wait until you see the high school," Agatha said. "I googled some pictures. Talk about keeping up with the Joneses. They're trying to keep up with Beacon City, and they're obsessed with being bigger and better. Only they don't have a fraction of the growth Beacon City is having. But they're spending like they are."

Hank adjusted his mirrors so he could see the fire station behind him.

"What are we doing?"

"Why? Are you afraid you're going to miss out on your date? What was that anyway?"

"Relax," Agatha said, buckling her seatbelt. "I was playing my part. Do you think he would've given us as much information as he had if it had been just you there? Two alphas squaring off against each other usually ends up with bloodshed and wounded egos. I just used what God gave me to speed things along without adding carnage to the mix."

"You sure were convincing," he said, sparing her a glance. He didn't know why he was so irritated. She was a grown woman, and she could do what she wanted. But still...it rankled a bit.

"Of course I was," she said. "It's not like he was hard on the eyes. But I'm not stupid. He was working the fire the night McCoy burned his house down. And he was right there when Kip Grogan dropped dead of a heart attack. So tell me, what are we doing?"

Hank sighed. Maybe he was overreacting. "We're flushing out the real killer. Because this whole thing screams of a cover up."

"He was pretty cool under fire though. But I caught what you were doing and how he was answering the questions. It's personal between him and McCoy," she said, pulling papers from her file. "He was the opposing quarterback those four years Gage cleaned their clocks in the Iron Pumpkin game."

"The plot thickens," Hank said.

"Speaking of plots." She turned to face him, but he

didn't take his eyes off the rearview mirror. He knew Tony was going to make a move, and he didn't want to miss it.

"I like working cases together, but if I can be honest, I'm also doing this to pay the bills. That includes your bill as well. It's great to catch a killer, but unless I know more about the process of the hunt that leads to the catch, then all we're doing is getting justice. Not that there's anything wrong with that," she said, before he could interrupt. "But I've been doing this a long time, and it's the insights I get from the cops I've worked with that make my characters so real. Does that make any sense?"

"Yes," Hank said. He didn't do well with conversation when he was irritated, and apparently he was still irritated about the way she and Tony interacted with each other. It was best to just let him cool off in silence for a while.

"How about we go grab the fire marshal?" she suggested.

"Or we could just follow Tony to him instead. Look there," he said, pointing behind him.

A big yellow pickup truck with Fire Chief emblazoned in red across the side slipped out of a bay.

"Huh," Agatha said. "How'd you know?"

"Gut feeling. Always listen to your gut. Unless you have food poisoning. Then it's usually best to stay home from work that day."

He backed out from in front of the police department and stayed a good distance away from the yellow truck.

"According to the GPS, the high school is just up ahead," she said.

"He's not going to the school. Too obvious. He's going to meet Chaffe where they can discuss our visit in person."

Agatha peered around the traffic and spotted a white SUV with red letters along the side. She assumed it was the fire marshal. Within a few yards, Tony began to break as the bright taillights flashed as strobes. He took a quick right without signaling. The two cars between them smashed on their brakes and hit the horn. Tony didn't bother looking back as he bounced the big truck over parking lot speed humps and around the rear of the Chinese restaurant.

"In there. Don't get too close," Agatha said excitedly.

"Haven't you been on a surveillance before?" Hank asked.

"No. Not really." She clapped. "I've been working cold cases for twenty years. Not really a lot of need for surveillance."

Hank followed them in the parking lot and went around to the side. All of a sudden, the yellow truck pulled out in front of them and Hank slammed on his brakes, stopping inches from the passenger side. There was a light tap on his bumper and a quick glance in the rearview mirror showed the fire marshal's SUV had pinned them in from the back.

Hank lifted his shirt and pulled his weapon from the holster. Agatha hit record on her phone's video.

"You can't be serious," he said, staring at her incredulously.

"I was going to..." and then she said, "Never mind. I was thinking of the book."

"Think of the book later. Let's think about getting out of here alive for now." He tapped the steering wheel lightly. "I knew we should've taken your Jeep. I'm not ramming them in this baby."

A voice sounded on a bullhorn behind them. "Passenger, exit the vehicle with your hands up."

Agatha gave him a concerned look and then did what she was instructed, backing her way toward Chafee's car.

"Driver," he said. "You're next."

Hank stayed where he was and was careful to move so they couldn't see him. The last thing he wanted was to end up with a bullet in the back of his head.

"Driver," Chafee said again. "I am ordering you out of the vehicle."

Hank opened the sun roof and held his badge up. He had little patience for bullies and even less tolerance.

"My name is Hank Davidson and I'm a special investigator, working on an active case. You are interfering in a criminal investigation." Hank held the badge higher. "Move your unit immediately."

The voice came back over the bullhorn and Hank rolled his eyes.

"I'm fire marshal, Peter Chaffe, and you're out of your jurisdiction. It's in your best interest to leave now."

"Idiots," Hank whispered to himself, and then he said aloud, "Let me make myself very clear. I'll have a whole swarm of cops here before you can blink, scrutinizing every move you make and going through every case you've ever had. Move your SUV now, or I'm getting out of this car and moving it myself."

"Why don't we talk this out," Chafee said. "Tony, why don't you move your truck so he can get through, and then we'll all have a chat."

Tony scowled at Hank, and then looked at Agatha with equal contempt, and he had to admit it put him in a much better mood. Hank pulled the car forward and in a position where they could get out easily, and he put his weapon back in his holster before getting out of the car. Agatha was waiting for him.

They walked to the alley behind the Chinese restaurant, and Hank felt the bile rise in the back of his throat. Agatha was looking very green. He had to stay in control.

These two would shoot him in the back if he wasn't careful.

"I appreciate you agreeing to talk to me," Hank said. "You're on my list of those to interview. Though I'm sure Tony told you that after he called you to tell you about our meeting."

"Now, just a minute here," Tony said. "You lied to me."

"There's no crime against that," Hank said. "I needed information and you told me a whole bunch more."

Tony took a step forward to try and intimidate him, but Hank stood his ground. Tony was a bully. He used his muscle to throw his weight around. But he wasn't used to being challenged.

"Do it," Hank said. "A little jail time might serve you well."

"Now, hold on here folks," Chafee said, his smile showing nicotine stained teeth. He held up his hands to try and dissolve the tension. "I think we just got off on the wrong foot. Tony, why don't you run on back to the station. I know you've got lots of work to do. I'll talk to these folks and then they can be on their way."

Chafee was a little guy, but had the posture of a banty rooster. He was several inches shorter than Agatha, so maybe about five-foot-eight, and he might have weighed a buck-fifty soaking wet. He suffered from eczema, but his ginger colored facial hair covered a lot of the dryness. His hair was sandy blonde and thinning, but he wore it long and brushed back to cover his scalp.

He smelled overwhelmingly of cigarettes, and the scent of him was almost strong enough to cover the days old Chinese food. *Almost.*

Hank smirked at Tony and knew he was all but waving a red flag in front of a bull, but Tony growled under his breath and turned and walked away. He got into his truck and sped off.

"Ma'am," Chafee said, looking at Agatha. "You don't look so good. Maybe we should go across the street to the coffee shop to have this discussion. You wouldn't want to pass out in this alley. No telling what's on the ground."

Hank watched Agatha closely and saw her swallow a few times, and he knew she wouldn't last much longer. The smell really was horrific. Worse than most of the crime scenes he'd worked. He grabbed her by the arm and steadied her, and then he hurried her toward the car.

"We'll meet you at the coffee shop," Hank called out, and then he whispered to Agatha, "Please don't throw up in my car."

CHAPTER EIGHT

The White Rhino Coffee House had a much better atmosphere than the alley behind the Chinese restaurant. It was in the middle of a strip mall and it looked crowded with the after church crowd.

Agatha had kept her eyes closed on the drive across the street and practiced some deep breathing exercises. Her skin was clammy, and the thought of smelling food or putting anything in her stomach wasn't sitting well.

"Sorry about that," she said. "I know I probably ruined your tough guy routine."

"Don't worry about it," Hank said. "It's not a routine."

Chafee parked several spots down from them, and she saw him flick a half of a cigarette to the ground when he got out. She wasn't a hundred percent yet, but she managed to get out of the car without falling over and to the door of the White Rhino. Hank held it open for her and she stepped into noise and chaos. But the smell of coffee didn't make her want to vomit, so that was a plus.

When Peter came in behind them it didn't go past her

notice that everyone stopped to look at him. A couple of people put cash on the table and got up to leave.

"Hey, Pete," a waitress said, handing them each a menu. "Let me clean off your usual table and you and your friends can sit down. Tuna salad is the special today."

Agatha gagged a little and Hank patted her on the back. It didn't take long for the table to get cleaned, and they took a seat in the corner booth. Hank guided her into the seat that faced the door and then he scooted in next to her.

"I've decided to give you folks my lunch break," Chafee said, showing his stained teeth again. "When I've paid my check that's the last I want to see or hear from y'all. Am I clear?"

"Not really," Hank said. "You can answer our questions, or I'll make a big scene as I arrest you for impeding our investigation. I like making big scenes. The messier the better."

Chafee paled and shifted in his seat. Agatha didn't move. This was a side of Hank she hadn't seen before. The big, scary side of Hank.

The waitress came up and Chafee ordered the special and a cup of coffee. Agatha ordered hot tea to soothe her stomach, and Hank stuck with coffee.

"How long have you and Tony known each other?" Hank asked.

"Everybody knows everybody around here. I watched him play high school ball. He was a heck of an athlete. Played quarterback."

"Did he play college ball, too?" Hank asked.

"Tony? Oh, no. He wanted to play awfully bad. Heck, we all thought he was on his way to becoming the next Roger Staubach, but the big four screwed him over. He went to a junior college in Mississippi to play ball, but he came back a month later because he was love sick. Turns out that his high school honey had met someone else while he was away. It didn't sit well."

"What's the big four?" Agatha asked. She knew the part of the story that she'd read, but she wanted to hear what they didn't print in the papers.

"Tony was the best quarterback this town had ever seen. They rarely lost a game. But he lost every year in the Pumpkin Bowl. No Rio Chino team before or since has ever lost four in a row. It was a black mark he couldn't remove."

"How horrible for a young boy to have that much pressure placed on him," she said, feeling sympathetic. "It's just a game after all."

"No, Tony didn't mind the pressure, but what he hated was the losing. And he could never win against Gage McCoy. Tony wound up losing everything as far as his chances at an athletic career. No one big would touch him after those four games. Didn't matter how well he played the rest of the season. He was never as good as McCoy. Being fire chief gave him the chance to reclaim his position as hometown hero."

"Wow, losing a game could really cost him his career?" Agatha asked.

"Remember Drew Bledsoe?" Hank asked.

"Who's Drew Bledsoe?"

"Do you know who Tom Brady is?"

"Him, I know," Agatha said.

"My point exactly," Hank said, and then he looked at Chafee to bring him back into the conversation. "What about you? Did you really think Tony had what it took to go all the way?"

Chafee shrugged. "I watched those games between Tony and McCoy, just like everyone else, and some kids just got what it takes. When McCoy and Tony were on the field, it's like Tony didn't even exist. McCoy was just that good. Any other game Tony shone like a beacon out there. But not against McCoy.

"Tony had what it took against all the other high school quarterbacks. It made him something of a celebrity in Rio Chino. He was a superstar. If anyone could've put us on the map it would've been him."

Agatha could hear the resentment in his voice and she raised her brows in surprise. Tony and Peter Chafee might work together, and they might be keeping each other's secrets, but there was no friendship there.

"The businesses boomed those years he played. The stadium was always full. And scouts and agents were always coming in. ESPN even sent a crew in a couple of times to get footage. But each year Gage McCoy beat him, those things started to fade away."

"That had to be rough on Tony," Agatha said. "For him to lose his dreams of football, go off to college, and then come home to find his girlfriend had hooked up with someone else. Most men would be pretty angry about life at that point."

Chafee chuckled and raised his coffee cup to be refilled. "Boy, would they. Tony was no different. He was over the moon for that girl. Followed her around like a puppy dog. Julie was gorgeous. You know when you live in a small town you sometimes have to adjust your idea of beauty because the pool is pretty shallow," he said, winking.

"I'm guessing that goes both ways?" Agatha asked.

"Huh?" Chafee asked, obviously confused.

"Never mind. You were talking about Tony and Julie."

"Oh, right. I think Tony just wanted her because she was the best, and he was that kid who was always a little bit entitled. He thought she should be falling all over herself to go out with him, but Julie always had a head on her shoulders. She was smart and serious, and she had big plans to go to SMU and get her law degree. Tony tried to get a scholarship so he could go there too, but they didn't want him to play football and he wasn't exactly a whiz when it came to academics.

"I don't suppose that Julie's new guy happened to be Gage McCoy?" Hank asked.

"Sure was," Chafee said. "Julie Dewey. She would've been better off with Tony because a decade later Gage up and killed her."

"What do you think set him off?" Hank asked.

"Who knows?" Chafee said. "Divorce will make a man crazy. I been through a couple myself and I'd be lyin' if I said I wouldn't have been real upset if something had happened to one of my exes.

"But McCoy never fit in here. How could he, being Beacon Hill's golden boy? But he loved Julie and she wanted to live close to her parents."

"Nick Dewey is her father?" Agatha asked.

"You know Nick?"

"We've spoken with him," Hank said vaguely. "How'd Gage get on with his father-in-law?"

"Fine, I guess. The Dewey's always had money, but it's not like McCoy was broke. He just didn't have no direction after his football career ended. As good as he was, he wasn't good enough to go pro. So he and Julie moved back here and Gage became a cop, and they set up house right in front of Tony."

Hank let out a low whistle. "Talk about rubbing salt in a wound."

"That it was," Chafee agreed.

"That would give Tony Fletcher the best motive and opportunity of anyone to set Gage McCoy up for murder. You were the one who ran that investigation, weren't you Chafee?"

Chafee sighed and sat back in the booth, feeling for the cigarettes in his front pocket. "Tony is a good politician. He's not a bad smoke eater, but he's better with the people than the fire hose. And everyone remembers him from back in the day. After old Kip died, Tony seemed to move right in as a natural for the job and the council appointed him in an emergency session to take over. To say that Tony was sorry Kip dropped dead would be a lie. It's the best thing that ever happened to him, and he didn't bother to hide his feelings of good fortune much."

"Who do you report to?" Hank asked.

"Tony," he said. "Everything goes through Tony. If he wants it, the council and the community just roll with it, even if the budget is tight. And to answer what I think your next question is going to be, yeah, Tony's the one who ordered me to investigate McCoy. It was so high profile he was involved in every step. He sat in on the statements of every witness and supervised all the reports I provided to the district attorney. Heck, he even came with me to the autopsy." Peter laughed a bit. "Thought he was going to lose it once the body was uncovered."

Agatha could only imagine what Julie McCoy looked like once she made it to the autopsy table, and she couldn't fault Tony for his reaction.

"Didn't the district attorney or the police chief object to you taking over the investigation? It seems highly inappropriate that a fire marshal would conduct a felony murder investigation when it involved their department." Hank asked.

Chafee shrugged again and took his cigarettes out of his pocket, tapping one out. She knew they wouldn't have much longer with him. His habit was calling him.

"What Tony wants, Tony gets. I didn't feel right about investigating the case, but technically I'm authorized to do so. But the RCFD was a victim of the crime, and there were a lot of emotions during those days. I asked Tony how it could be ethical for me to investigate McCoy. But he didn't care. I turned my reports into Tony, and then I never saw them again. He's the one who had direct contact with the DA. Gage decided to take a plea deal instead of facing the death penalty. It seemed pretty cut and dried from there. Who would take a plea deal if they were innocent?"

"What was your opinion?" Hank asked.

"I honestly don't know why he took the deal. The evidence didn't stack up. There was no concrete proof of anything. I went to the chief of police and to the DA, but both of them told me there was no course for appeal since Gage had pled guilty. The people here needed someone to be guilty, and there was no use stirring stuff up once Gage took the deal. You're the first person who's asked me about it in ten years."

"How did Julie end up handcuffed to the bed?" Agatha asked.

"The easy explanation is that Gage cuffed her there and set the fire. It wasn't a sophisticated arson. He used the coffee maker as a delayed starter so he could get to work. Then he attended the sergeant's shift briefing before the blaze could be detected, giving him a room full of people to alibi him."

"Was that your independent conclusion?" Hank asked.

"Yeah, it's a classic mistake that people make when trying to be tricky. It's a good try, but not good enough to fool anyone with any experience. I have proof of how it was done, but not necessarily who did it. I'm not sure we would've solved it if he hadn't confessed. You're always going to look at the spouse first and hardest. You know that," he said, looking to Hank. "And maybe we could've made something stick, but the fact is, someone cuffed Julie to the bed, shot her in the house, and then set the house on fire. It wasn't exactly a genius move as far as trying to cover up the scene of the crime. Honestly, I figured if someone like Gage was going to commit murder, he'd do a heck of a lot better job not getting caught. He was a sharp guy."

The word confessed stuck in Hanks's mind. He'd use it when the time was right.

"Where was the boy?" Agatha asked.

"At the football game with friends. That's the shame of it there. That boy's life was never the same. I know his grandfather up and moved them all over to Beacon City, and the kid's following in his father's footsteps. The game Friday night is going to be tense, for more than one reason."

"Did Gage really hold the firemen at bay with a shotgun?" Hank asked.

"Who knows? There was so much chaos that night. I never talked to anyone who confessed to actually seeing one. Tony swore he had firefighters call him on the radio to complain about the weapon, but he didn't know who and nobody spoke up. It didn't make sense for Gage to let the place burn down. When I interviewed him, before he confessed, he said he and Julie were back together. That they'd worked everything out."

"You said twice now that Gage confessed, but you side stepped saying he confessed to you." Hank slid it into the conversation.

Chaffe averted his look. His fingers tapped at the packet of cigarettes in his pocket.

"Tony said he heard him say it. I was told to document it."

Hank squeezed his fists into tight knots. He hated injustice, but he had to remain cool.

"So how in the world did Gage get charged for the murder of Kip Grogan's death?" Agatha asked. "Everything I've been able to find said it was a heart attack."

"Ever played pile on as a kid?" Chafee asked. "What better way to make Gage out to be the bad guy. I bet no one even remembers Julie's name, but no one forgets Kip."

"You remember her," Agatha said.

"I remember the victims," he said. "I'm not saying I haven't made mistakes. I have. And this was one of them. But my hands were tied, and there's nothing I can do. Everyone got what they wanted."

"Except Gage McCoy and his son," Hank said.

"Why were Gage and his wife getting divorced?" Agatha said, something prompting her to ask the question.

"Well, seems like Gage was better at being a QB than being faithful. Of course, it didn't take long before Tony showed himself as the good friend and started working on getting Julie back. It was a mess." Chafee rolled his eyes and signaled for the check. "Her dad, Nick, had a heart-to-heart with Julie and Gage and laid things out for them. He convinced them to get into counseling and give it another shot."

"How did Tony take that?" she asked.

"How do you think?" he asked. "He lost against McCoy again. That was six for six."

CHAPTER NINE

TUESDAY

"Long time, no see, stranger," Penny said when Agatha walked into the Kettle Café two days later. "That hottie you managed to wrangle is at the back table."

Agatha gritted her teeth. Penny was a fan, which she didn't mind, but she was beginning to become somewhat of an irritant. Agatha treasured her privacy, and maybe everyone in town did know more about her than she thought, but at least they had the decency not to mention it. Not Penny though. She made it a point to let Agatha know she knew her business, whether it was true or not.

Agatha decided the best thing to do was ignore her, and she looked around the café and saw Hank in the back booth. There was a woman sitting across from him wrapped up in a scarf, but she couldn't tell who it was from the back.

"Morning, partner," Hank said, smiling at her as she came up to the table.

"Good morning," she said. And then she caught a glimpse of the woman as she turned to face Agatha.

"Well as I live and breathe," Heather said, raising a brow. "I was wondering if I'd ever see you again."

Heather Cartwright had been Agatha's best friend since grade school. They were total opposites in every way, but somehow their friendship worked. Heather was selfish and self-absorbed, but she was generous in giving to others and she had a good heart. She'd been married five times over the course of the last twenty years, and there was something inside her friend that was a little bit sad and a little bit broken, but it was hard to see unless you really knew her.

She and Heather hugged fiercely and then Agatha scooted into the booth across from Hank. It had been a few weeks since she'd seen Heather due to finishing up her book.

"I missed you," Heather said. "I've needed to talk to you about a hundred times. You've missed out on a lot. Let's do dinner tomorrow night, okay? Brisket Basket. Meat plate special."

"It's a date. You know I love meat," she said, winking at Hank. "I'll leave you two to your crime solving now that I've gotten what I came for. Thanks for the coffee, Sugar." She blew Hank a kiss and waved goodbye to Agatha.

"She's exhausting," Hank said, smiling.

"Which is exactly what her ex-husbands always say."

"We've got a meeting with the Rio Chino coroner today," he said. "The name is Dr. Anna Rusk."

"Sounds good. You know I'm always happy to eat." She pressed at her swollen eyes. She'd had a rough couple of nights since meeting with Peter Chafee. "I've been thinking a lot about our talk with Chafee."

"Yeah, me too," Hank said. "Penny can I get more coffee, please? You want something?"

"Hot tea. Strong and black. There's something that's

been bugging me about him, as helpful as he seemed to be. But he's waited ten years, and all of a sudden he just decides to spill his guts and be helpful because two strangers come to town asking questions? Only after he and Tony tried to intimidate us out of town first."

"You did a good job questioning him," Hank answered. "He was more receptive to you because he saw you as non-threatening. But profiling people like him is what I've done for most of my career. He's pretty textbook. It's a simple case of him giving us a surface appearance. Only letting us see what he wants us to see. But that doesn't fill out the profile accurately."

Penny took that moment to bring her tea and Hank's refill. "Are y'all solving a new crime? You've got that serious look about you. I can't wait to read about it in whatever book you're writing, Agatha. Maybe your investigator will have a new love interest." Penny waggled her eyebrows, not being subtle about the hint at all.

Agatha felt heat creep up the side of her neck, and she narrowed her eyes at Penny. But she'd turned around to put down the coffee pot.

"Are y'all wanting breakfast this morning?"

"Not for me," Hank said.

"Me either," Agatha said. Between her exhaustion and the grumpiness from dealing with Penny, she was starting to think it was unwise for her to leave her house.

"What's going on with you?" Hank asked.

"I don't know. I think this one is just getting to me. A lot of people are suffering because of decisions that were made. I keep thinking of the kid. It's not easy to lose your parents as an adult. I can't imagine what it's been like for him. I've been thinking about my own for the past couple of days. It's been a long time since the grief of their deaths has hit me this strong, but this case is bringing it back." She said.

Hank reached out and took her hand, and she marveled at the size and strength of it. And the comfort.

"Mine died when I was a boy," he said. "And you're right, it's not easy, no matter what age you are. And you never get over it. I don't think we're supposed to. But the grief softens over time. And the memories become sweeter."

She felt the tears start to well in her eyes and blinked them back rapidly. There was no time for this today. She cleared her throat and squeezed his hand, and then pulled back. "Thank you," she said. "Sorry about that. You were telling me about your thoughts on Chafee."

"Don't ever apologize," he said. "That's what partners are for. Like I was saying, the guy's an interesting case, but without a better file on him and his background, I can't tell with more than about eighty-five percent accuracy that he was telling the truth. His profile shows loyalty, service and martyrdom. Which loosely means Chaffe is all in all, a decent man, but one who isn't going to go out on his own to bring down Tony. He doesn't have the leadership skills or alpha personality. He wants to...but he falls short."

"You think Tony did it?"

"I know he did," Hank said. "We just have to prove it."

She'd dug up every report she could find on the arson investigation and gotten copies since they'd made their visit to Rio Chino. She passed the file across to Hank. Agatha didn't need to read them. She'd practically memorized every word on the pages.

"How are we going get Tony to fess up?" she asked.

"Tony is a full-blown egomaniac with narcissistic traits. This job as fire chief is the best thing he's ever accomplished, and it's the only thing that gives him purpose.

Unfortunately, Tony's in a strike three predicament. The first was his football career. The second was Julie. And if he gets caught up in this whole thing it'll be strike three. He's not going to voluntarily give that up. No way he'll confess." Hank snarled.

"We could interview everyone who was at the scene," she said. But the look on Hank's face was skeptical. "Yeah, I guess they're not going to talk. Especially with Tony being chief. But there has to be someone he's afraid of. Someone who can upset his apple cart."

"But who?" Hank sipped at his drink.

Agatha exhaled, "Yeah, I guess they're not talking. There has to be someone who can help rattle Tony."

"Nick," Hank said, snapping his fingers.

"But I thought you and he weren't..."

"Friends? The jury is still out on that. I don't like being used. But he's a man who wants answers more than we do. He's a grieving father. He'll do whatever he can to help us. Though it would've gone a long way for him to just be upfront with me."

"Maybe he didn't want you to feel pressured," Agatha said. "Or maybe he was waiting to get to know you first to see if he could trust you."

"Maybe," Hank said, considering.

He glanced down at the file of papers in front of him and started flipping through them. "What's this?"

"It's the jail's intake inventory and receipt for Gage on the night of his arrest."

"They arrested him at the scene of the fire, right?" Distracted, Hank asked.

"Yep."

"The correctional officer confiscated everything from

McCoy before placing him in a holding cell, right?" Hank asked.

He was onto something.

"That's their policy."

"Look here at the inventory list receipt." He turned the paper so she could see too.

She'd looked over the inventory list probably a dozen times. "I see a list of clothing and equipment. What are you seeing that I'm not?"

"This is McCoy's duty rig. You know, his police utility belt," Hank said. "One leather police belt. One Velcro under belt. One holster. One magazine holder. Two Glock 23 magazines. Fifteen bullets in each magazine. One handcuff pouch. One set of Smith and Wesson hinged handcuffs.

One Taser holster. One police baton holder. One police mace holder. Four leather Velcro belt keepers. NOTE: Items confiscated on scene of the arrest for officer safety, and transferred to jail booking officer: One Glock 23 9mm pistol, serial number GMP230311659mm. One Taser, serial number TXJ698734. One Monadnock expandable police baton. One can of police freeze +P mace."

"All that fits on a police belt?" Agatha asked.

"Yep. That's what the belt keepers are for. To hold your pants up," he said, smiling.

"Wow, it must wreak havoc on the hips."

"Especially with his cuffs still on the belt. What did they find attached to Julie and the bed?"

Agatha's eyes widened. "Oh. Handcuffs."

CHAPTER TEN

"There's something about this town that seems familiar," Agatha said as they drove past the Rio Chino city limits. "I just can't put my finger on it."

They kept watch for Tony and his yellow truck as they motored through town. The coroner's office was at the end of Kip Grogan Avenue. It also doubled as the town's morgue and funeral parlor. Austin stone exteriors, common through the state of Texas, adorned the older building. It was obvious that not all public services got the royal treatment or the new construction.

They parked and headed inside, and Agatha shivered as a cold blast of air greeted them. A young receptionist was typing away at her desk, and she looked up at them and smiled, her fingers never stopping.

"Are y'all here to see the doc?" she asked. Her name tag said Beth.

"Yes, she's expecting us. Hank Davidson and Agatha Harley."

"Why's it so cold in here?" Agatha asked.

The girl chuckled. "This is normal. It was in the job description. It's why I'm dressed like a polar bear."

"How long you been working here?" Hank asked

"Two days. Let me buzz the Doc for you."

Agatha could hear the click of heels coming down the hallway, and a few seconds later there was a beep and a set of double doors automatically opened. She recognized Anna Rusk from the research photos she'd grabbed off the internet, but the photos didn't do her justice.

She was tall and was probably in her early forties, though she could pass for a decade younger. Her eyes were striking, emerald in color and slightly tilted at the ends, giving her a mermaid-like appearance. She was mixed-race and her dark hair was cropped closely around her face in a pixie cut.

Agatha watched Hank out of the corner of her eye. He was mesmerized. She couldn't blame him. The doc was a knockout.

"Hello" she said, holding out a hand first to Agatha and then to Hank. "I'm Dr. Rusk. But please call me Anna. I'm assuming you're my lunch dates?"

"We appreciate you meeting with us," Hank said.

"Well, you offered to buy lunch," she said, grinning. "Who's going to turn down that kind of deal."

Agatha liked her immediately. She had an easy-going personality and had that innate ability to put people at ease. "Should we walk across the street? I saw a place to eat."

"Well, I'm sure not getting in a car with two strangers," she said.

Hank flashed his badge. "We're actually conducting an investigation into the death of Julie McCoy."

Rusk rolled her eyes.

"Is that a problem?" Agatha asked.

Rusk didn't offer a reply right away, so they walked across the street to the little Mexican restaurant.

"I didn't work that case," she said. "I didn't move to the area until a couple of years later, but it was still all anyone talked about. I've only heard second-hand what went on during the investigation, and I still can't explain why they did some of the things they did. You see a lot of strange things in small, underfunded towns. And you see a lot of unqualified people do the best they can with the skills they have. I'm very good at what I do," she said, smiling unashamedly. "They're lucky to have me."

"Who are the *them* you're referring to?" Hank asked.

"Chief Fletcher mostly. He couldn't wait to tell anyone who would listen about the folks from Philly looking to stir up the McCoy case again. He warned us you might be around to talk and to be nice," she said, bearing her teeth. "Even said he got you sidelines to the big game so you can see how hospitable we all are here."

"I can assure you," Hank said, "I can't be bribed. And we're not here *looking* to stir up the case again. We *are* stirring up the case again. From what we can see, there were mistakes all around. Malicious, intentional mistakes."

Hank opened the door of the restaurant and Agatha followed Anna inside. Mexican food was her weakness, and the smell of homemade tortillas had her mouth watering.

Rusk smirked and raised a brow. "One of you is lying. Wonder who it is?"

"We're only interested in the truth," Agatha said.

They followed the hostess to a table and sat down, and they were immediately served with chips and salsa. They gave their order before resuming the conversation.

"You're not from Philly," Anna said, staring at Agatha. "You're a Texas girl. So there's one lie right there."

"Fletcher didn't ask Agatha the question," Hank said. "I'm the one from Philly. Born and raised. Spent twenty-six years on the job there."

"Yeah, I can hear it in your voice," she said. "I'm from Clifton Heights."

"Seventy-Sixers fan?" Hank asked.

She grinned. "It's the only basketball game in town. You cannot imagine how good it is to meet someone from back home. This town has gotten on my last nerve."

"I completely understand. I actually moved here on purpose too." Hank laughed. "Well, not *here*. I'm about an hour away in Rusty Gun."

Rusk grimaced, "Oh, I'm so sorry."

Agatha felt very much like a third-wheel. No wonder Hank had been so irritated when she and Tony had flirted a little.

"It's not so bad," Hank said. "It's a nice little town. But it was a big change from the city."

"I can imagine. Watching the grass grow is about all there is to do. You look like a guy who likes to be in the middle of the action."

Agatha couldn't help it. She rolled her eyes. She dipped another chip into her salsa. It's like she wasn't even there.

"Which is why I'm asking for your help in this," Hank said.

She sighed and waited to answer until the waitress had finished putting their food in front of them.

"Look, Hank. I like you guys. And I believe you. I'm no dummy. I know what I'm dealing with. I'm still amazed they hired a black Yankee to do this job, and believe me, it hasn't exactly been easy. I'll do what I can to help you, but they've got that case locked down pretty tight."

"You mean it's a solid investigation?" Agatha asked.

"No, I mean they've restricted access to almost everyone except the prosecutor and fire chief. I tried to review the case several years back when people were still talking about it. All I have access to are the handwritten notes and a few pics that were buried on the old coroner's desktop computer. He probably didn't know they were there. He wasn't the most technologically advanced."

"It's a start," Hank said. "Let's finish eating and take a look at what you've got."

AN HOUR later they were back at the walk-in freezer where Rusk worked. She said hello to Beth and then badged them through to the long hallway that led to her office.

"I've got everything right here," Rusk said, digging in the bottom of her desk drawer for a file. She handed it to Agatha and then moved the computer mouse so the screen-saver cleared. She clicked on a desktop folder and images appeared. "I'll also save them onto a jump drive for you."

"May I?" Agatha asked, pointing to the empty conference table.

"Be my guest. I'll make copies for you to take back."

Agatha thanked her as she cracked open the files at a conference table near the narrow window opening. She felt the twinge in her gut as she saw the first autopsy image. She loved the study, but hated what murder did to the person.

"Dr. Rusk, I see in the autopsy that a blood sample was taken and showed zero carboxyhemoglobin. I also see that there was no smoke inhalation present in her lungs, or inhalation damage, or laryngospasm. There were no thermal injuries in her airways, or soot in her esophagus or stomach." Agatha asked

"That's right." Rusk agreed.

"There are notations of multiple ligature marks on her body. Was there more than the one handcuff, or were those ligatures created by the heat-splitting of the body against clothing or jewelry?" Agatha asked.

"You know your stuff," Rusk said, brows raised. "You a cop?"

"A mystery writer," Agatha said with a smile. "And it helps I almost had a forensic anthropology degree before I quit to write full time. I'm good at what I do. Just like you."

Anna nodded, respect in her eyes. "There was only the one handcuff, but it wasn't needed to keep her in place. There was no blood or bruising where the cuff had been snapped against her wrist."

"It was for show," Hank said. "Unnecessary."

"Exactly," Rusk said.

"Cause of death was a GSW at close range to the heart," Agatha continued. "The bullet's trajectory looks to have been a steep, up to down angled path." She squinched her nose in confusion, trying to see it in her mind.

"Julie was shot while sitting on the bed, but whoever was standing over her was pretty tall to cause that angle of entry," Hank said.

"Maybe even as tall as Tony," Agatha added.

"Whoa!" Rusk said. "Y'all think Chief Fletcher killed this girl?"

"Just got to prove it," Hank said. "That's the fun part."

"I really hope you're as good at your job as you say you are because it's going to take some creativity to clear the man whose been sitting in prison the last ten years."

"The handcuffs," Hank said.

"Handcuffs?" Rusk asked.

"Yeah, is there a picture of them from the crime scene?"

Agatha shifted through the pages in the file, but there was nothing there.

"Doc?" Hank asked. "What about you?"

Rusk was already at her desktop clicking through the images. Hank moved to stand behind her.

"Will this do?" Her eyes glistened in the florescent lighting.

"Aggie," Hank said. "Look here. What do you see?"

"A handcuff." She said and she leaned closer. "A chained handcuff, single blade. Good catch."

She patted Hank on the shoulder.

"Anna, where would this handcuff be stored?" Hank asked.

Rusk furrowed her brow in thought and pulled a large three-ring binder from a book shelf, dropping it on the conference table.

"As I feared," she said. "The prosecutor probably has it."

"Probably?" Hank challenged.

"Policy says all evidence upon conviction shall remain with the prosecution in the event of post-conviction relief, retrial or appeal," Rusk said, reading the policy aloud.

"Is that bad?" Agatha asked.

"If he won't allow me to peek at the fire investigator's reports, you think he's going to let you inspect evidence?"

CHAPTER ELEVEN

WEDNESDAY

"Hey, Nick," Hank said as he greeted the man at the Kettle Café. It was good to be back in Rusty Gun, which he thought he'd never say. But the place was starting to grow on him, and Rio Chino gave him the creeps.

Nick shook his hand and said, "I saw you called yesterday, but I had no cell service out at the 777."

Hank had already gotten them a table since he'd arrived first.

"You didn't have to chopper to meet me."

Nick laughed as he peered through the Kettle café's window. "Are you kidding me? I never miss an opportunity to ride in that thing. Heck of a lot faster than a car. Besides, I figured I owed you another apology for..."

"Stop," Hank said. "No need to apologize. I know the truth. And I want to say again how sorry I am about this whole thing. Your family has suffered like no one should because of one man's jealousy." Hank saw the moisture in Nick's eyes and the tear roll down his cheek. "Why didn't you just level with me?"

"Habit, I guess. I've begged for over eight years for the truth. I got nowhere. No one, and I mean no one, was willing to lift a finger to help me. I know it's petty, but I was sure it had something to do with my leaving Rio Chino and moving to Beacon City. Heck, it's where I grew up. This stupid football rivalry has that town insane. Worst part about it, no one in Beacon City even cares, and everyone in Rio Chino is just trying to cover their own behinds."

"Who have you asked for help?

"Hank, it's no secret. I'm loaded rich. I went to everybody from the governor to the school crossing guard. That fire department is as crooked as an unpressurized hose."

"You were never convinced Gage could have killed your daughter?" Hank asked.

"No way in the world that boy killed her. He loved her. Sure, he messed up, but so did she. I had a good talking to them, and they decided to stick it out and get some help."

"Then what?"

"It was that jealous idiot fireman. Tony Fletcher. He'd been a loser to Gage all his life, and he couldn't accept losing to him again."

"Nick, can I tell you something? But I swear if you whisper a word to those rich cronies, this case ends."

"Hank, this is my daughter we're talking about. And most importantly, my grandson. The boy has lost his mother. His dad is not responsible."

"I think I can prove Tony did it. Or at least that Gage didn't do it."

"How?" Nick asked, a spark of hope in his eyes.

"I can't tell you, but I do need your help."

"Anything," Nick agreed. "I'll give up everything I own."

"I know you would. I need access to a piece of evidence,

and the District Attorney has it in his possession. Is there any way possible to convince him to allow me access? All I need is a moment."

"I don't think so," Nick said. "We're not what you'd call on friendly terms."

"How about the police chief? No one has even mentioned his name. Was he here at the time? Think he could help?"

"Doubt it. The police chief at the time tried to have the Texas Rangers come in and investigate. Can you guess what happened?"

"New chief?"

"Yep. The mayor fired him for insubordination the very next week. Had the prosecutor threaten to press charges unless he agreed to go back to San Antonio. The next day, he and his family packed up and disappeared."

"So what do we do? I'm an outsider here, so you're going to have to take the lead on this one."

"We've got a newly elected governor, and I contributed a heck of a lot of money to his campaign. I wouldn't mind making another donation if he'll put the pressure on."

Hank nodded. "Let me know how it goes. Aggie and I will head back to Rio Chino this afternoon. Maybe a cold call will get us through."

"I really appreciate you doing this, and I'm sorry I didn't square with you from the start. I just didn't want you to feel pressured because it was my daughter. And honestly, I had no clue who you were when we met."

Hank shook his hand, and decided to put it behind them. He enjoyed Nick's company.

"We'll get to the bottom of this," Hank said. "No matter what it takes."

Hank waited until Nick left and then got Agatha's

attention. She'd been sitting on the other side of the restaurant to see how things went.

"He's going to see the governor," Hank said.

"Think he'll come through?" She asked.

"It's a long shot."

Sheriff Coil came through the door of the café and spotted them immediately.

"Sheriff," Hank said, shaking the other man's hand.

"How's it going, Hank? Agatha?"

"You know, I keep my ear to the ground. I know what y'all are up to," Coil said, sliding into the booth where Nick had just been.

"Meaning?" Agatha bit.

"I've been hearing y'all are stirring up trouble in Rio Chino," Coil said. "If it's what I suspect it to be, I'd say y'all were on the right track. I know this case well. I was sent into try and help since they didn't have any experience dealing with these kinds of crimes. They didn't let us stick around for long. The trick is going to be getting access to evidence."

"Yes, so why haven't you offered to help before now?" Agatha scolded him.

"You never asked. I mean, you are my special investigator, Hank. Least you could've done is let me know. And I guess you don't mind flashing that badge around so much now, do you?"

Agatha snickered. "He's got you there, Hank. I've seen more of that badge than I've seen my own home in the last few days."

"I can't get directly involved, but I can try getting you limited access to records."

"How about evidence?" Hank asked.

"Like what?"

"Handcuffs. The ones found on Julie's wrist after the fire."

"It's going to be tough. I'll work on it." Coil shook his head to move the hair out of his face.

A glimmer of an idea started to form in Hank's mind, and he snapped his finders. "The pistol."

"You need a pistol?" Coil reached for his backup weapon.

"No." Hank waved his hands. "No."

"What?" Agatha asked.

"Julie was shot with a .45 caliber pistol. Gage McCoy carried a 9mm. They confiscated it from him on scene," Hank said.

"Drop gun used," Agatha interrupted.

"Let the man process his thoughts, writer girl," Coil said good-naturedly.

"Firemen don't carry weapons, and Tony was never reported to carry or possess a firearm. If Tony did kill Julie, where did he get the .45, and what did he do with it after?" Hank continued.

"Good questions," Agatha said.

"I just remembered that while reading the radio transmissions transcripts someone said something over an open mic about hand me my gun," Hank said. "From the chronology of the radio traffic, my guess would be that was Kip ordering someone to get his pistol so he could stop Gage from interfering."

"What type of weapon did Kip have?" Agatha asked.

"I'll run a records check for licensed gun owners and pistol range memberships," Coil said. "While you're back in Rio Chino, stop by the county 911 commission. They hold onto those recordings for at least ten years. You might be lucky and they still have them. The DA has a copy for the case file, but you aren't getting near them. I'm sure you can sweet talk a 911 operator into letting you listen to a recording."

"Thanks, Coil," Hank said. "We find that .45, and we can pin the killer."

"You think Kip killed Julie?" Agatha asked. "I thought we were looking at Tony."

"We need to look at whoever had access to the command post, and who had access to Kip's weapon."

"Chafee told us Tony was in the command post with Kip. Tony has to be the one who Kip was asking to hand him his pistol."

"Y'all just gotta find that .45," Coil said.

"Yeah, after eight years, it'll be just that easy," Hank said sarcastically.

"You know," Coil said. "You stink at being retired, so I guess you might as well spend your time looking for a gun. It is the key."

"Key to what?" Agatha asked.

"Another man's freedom."

CHAPTER TWELVE

"I'M SURE GETTING TIRED OF THIS DRIVE TO RIO Chino," Agatha said.

"At least the food has been good," Hank said. "And some of the company."

Agatha rolled her eyes again. She was sure he was talking about Dr. Rusk. But she couldn't complain too much. Hank was a great character study for the hero of her next novel. Hank was anything but a typical cop, and she'd really enjoyed getting to see another side of him for this case. The tougher side of him. She had a feeling when Hank wasn't acting "retired," his middle name might be Trouble.

"What do you think of Dr. Rusk?" Hank asked.

"She's pretty, and I think she likes you. You should probably ask her to the dance."

"Aggie, this isn't junior high school. I meant, do you think she's legit about her suspicions or just do you think maybe she's in on it with the others and trying to string us along?"

Agatha shrugged. "I didn't get that vibe from her. She

seemed like a straight shooter. But she could probably get in a lot of trouble for helping us as much as she did. Though it might not matter. I got the feeling she doesn't plan on sticking around Rio Chino much longer. She seems like a city girl."

"Probably so." Hank agreed. "So, you think she likes me?" He looked at her with mischief in his eyes and she smacked him on the shoulder.

"Yeah, I don't think you need any help feeding your ego. I'm staying silent on this one."

"That would be a first," he said. "I sure hope Nick or Coil come through. The gun totally slipped my mind. I got fixated on the handcuff angle and slipped on the obvious."

"Hiding in plain sight," Agatha said.

"Retirement is kicking my butt. Making me slow and lazy."

"Look on the bright side, at least your retirement wardrobe has improved. I wasn't sure how much more I could take with you wearing those black socks and Birkenstocks while you watered your roses."

"That's all your doing. With what you pay me as a consultant I can afford to hire a gardener."

"You're welcome. Are heading over to the 911 center?" she asked.

"Might as well. I think we should try getting Chafee to meet us out there to ask him about the .45. I just got a feeling that the closer we get to Friday night's kickoff that the less help we'll get from Chafee. Old loyalties, even if he despises Tony, run deep."

"I'll text him." She whipped out her cell phone and began typing.

She watched as they avoided Kip Grogen Avenue and

took a different way to the 911 center. "Where are we going?"

"If you haven't noticed, there aren't a whole lot of BMWs in this town. I thought it best we avoid driving by the fire station. It'd be like waving a red flag in front of Tony."

It took them an extra fifteen minutes to get to the 911 center. The building was newly constructed and almost as modern and shiny as the fire department.

"Crap," she said.

"What?" Hank asked.

"This place remind you of anywhere? What do you want to bet everyone in here is loyal to Tony? He got them a new building they probably can't afford." She exclaimed.

"Let's see how it goes." He smirked, "Time to charm."

Hank opened the door for her and she thanked him. She was an independent woman, but she appreciated good manners. The lobby was as advanced as the fire department's entrance. There was a small bust of Kip Grogan in one corner, and a giant portrait painting of Tony on the opposite side. There was no equal portrait of the police chief.

"What is wrong with this town?" she asked.

"Too many things to ask."

"Hank," someone called out.

Agatha turned at the sound of the familiar voice. "What in the world?"

Deputy Karl Johnson waved at them from across the room and jogged toward them. He was about her height, but he'd bulked up with muscle over the past few years. His skin was the color of dark chocolate. She still saw him as the boy she once babysat. In her mind, he was still way too young to be driving, much less carrying a firearm.

"Whew, is it good to see a familiar face," he said.

There were quite a few officers milling about in the lobby from different cities, but they all looked like cops in the tactical pants and polos that had their city's name over the breast or on the sleeve.

"What's going on?" Hank asked as they stepped away from a larger group of officers.

"Sheriff Coil sent me for NCIC certification. I have to have training before I can request information through the National Crime Information Center's database."

"Great training certification, Karl. I couldn't have done anything without access to NCIC. How many days is the class?"

"Three days. This is the last day. They said it wouldn't be safe around here on Friday for the big game. The instructor said Friday was for Rio Chino alumni only. She might've been joking or not, but I'm not taking any chances. This place is a little nutty." He looked around the lobby, his eyes wide. "I'm just ready to get home."

"Who's that?" Agatha asked, nodding toward a woman trying to get Karl's attention.

"Speaking of nutty," he said on an exhale. "She's one of the instructors. She tried to shove her number down the front of my pants yesterday. Just caught her before things got embarrassing for both of us. This place is like a different planet."

"Hey, Mr. Irresistible," Agatha said. "You think you could help us out by using your charm?"

"Maybe," Karl said. "The sheriff told me you guys were investigating something up here and that I might run into you. What do you have in mind?"

"We need information, and we don't think they're very likely to help us out." Agatha slipped Karl the paper where she'd written the date, time, and file number of the 911 transcript they needed. If he could sweet talk his instructor, the information would lead to the recording from the night McCoy was arrested.

Lights flashed in the lobby and Karl explained that meant class was back in session.

"I'll do my best on this," he said. "Catch y'all later."

"Hello, may I help you?" a lady with a name tag that read Corky greeted them.

"Hi there," Agatha said. "I'm Agatha, and this is Hank. We're Karl's parents." Hank stepped on her toe and she bit her bottom lip to keep from yelping.

The girl looked confused. As she probably should have at that announcement, but it had been the first thing that had come to mind.

"It's so nice to meet you. Karl just told us all about you. He said you're one of the best instructors he's ever had."

The woman tossed her blonde hair over her shoulder and beamed at them.

"Wow, really? He's just the sweetest thing."

"I think he's got a crush," Agatha went on. "He never talks to us about women. You must be something special."

The woman blushed as red as the instructor's shirt she was wearing.

"Did Karl get a chance to speak to you about the favor he needed?" Hank asked.

She looked confused. "Favor? No, but we've been so busy we really haven't had much time to talk. I'm happy to help however I can though."

"I'm sure he'd appreciate that," Hank said. "Why don't you invite him to dinner tonight. He said this is his last night here."

"Oh, that's a great idea," she said. "Do you know what the favor is?"

"We're looking for a recording of a tape, and someone told us to check here. Karl's cousin's voice is on the tape, and since he's no longer with us, I know it'd mean a lot for Karl to get a copy of it. They were very close. Like brothers."

"Do you have the date or log number so I can look it up?"

"You bet," Agatha said, jotting it down quickly on a torn piece of paper from her purse.

"Y'all hang tight," Corky said. "I'll be right back."

Hank whistled once she'd gone off. "That was way too easy."

"Never underestimate a desperate woman who's just a little bit crazy. You could see it in her eyes."

"A little bit crazy?" Hank said. "If I saw a woman looking at me the way she's looking at Karl, I'd run screaming in the opposite direction."

"Yeah, right," Agatha said, snorting out a laugh. "That woman was hot. Men will put up with a lot of crazy for sex. They just don't want to end up marrying them."

Hank's lips twitched. "No wonder you write such believable characters."

"Thanks, but I kinda feel guilty."

Hank raised his hands, "About what?"

"Karl." She chuckled.

CHAPTER THIRTEEN

"Hank, how can this car not have a CD player?"

"I don't know, why would it? Who listens to CDs anymore." Hank stabbed at the buttons on the dashboard. "That's like asking why I don't have an 8-track tape player."

"Funny," Agatha said. "Here comes Chafee. I bet he's got one we can use."

"Don't even think about asking him. We don't want anyone to know we have this."

"Geez, I was kidding. This isn't my first rodeo, cowboy."

They climbed out of the BMW as Chafee approached. They'd decided to meet about five miles out of town near a livestock barn. Hank hated the idea because it would be just a matter of minutes until his allergies made an appearance. Agatha handed him a handkerchief, anticipating the attack like a good partner.

"Hi, Peter," Agatha said, holding out her hand to Chafee.

Peter didn't look so good. His eyes were concealed behind oversized sunglasses, and he looked nervous. It didn't take an experienced cop to understand they were being monitored in some way. Hank put on his own sunglasses on so he could move his eyes undetected as he looked for company along the lone stretch of highway. He also made sure his weapon was immediately accessible.

"Well, if it's not Harley and Davidson," Chafee said, tugging at his shirt collar. "Funny seeing you two out here. Having car trouble?"

Since they'd invited Chafee to meet them out there, Agatha raised her brows at the statement.

"It's a good thing you passed by when you did," Hank said. "There's no cell service out here either."

Agatha noticed how tight the muscles were in Hank's jaw were. His lips had drawn into a thin line across his face and she knew his senses were on high alert. His elbow kept in contact with the pistol strapped to his right side. Hank was angry, but alert for ambush. He signaled behind him and Agatha took it as a sign to move back toward the car. She moved to the driver's side in case they needed to make a quick escape.

Hank's signals to Chafee were slow and purposeful. He had no choice but to see where Chafee's loyalties lied. His left hand lifted to his chest before he pointed to his ear, and then his eyes, and finally he used his thumb to point to his ear while his index finger aimed at his eye.

Chafee nodded and reached up to take off his glasses. When he did he carefully pointed to his ear.

Audio only. Which meant they didn't have other eyes on them. She grabbed her iPad and a stylus from Hank's car and returned to the two men. Since they couldn't talk openly, they'd write it out.

"How can I help y'all? I was on my way over to the stadium to make sure it's ready for Friday night's game."

Agatha wrote her question on the iPad and handed it to Chafee.

Do firemen carry weapons on duty?"

Chaffe shook his head in the negative.

"There's something going on with the engine," Hank said. "When I crank her up steam starts coming out of the hood. Do you know anything about cars?"

"Sure do," Chafee said. "Why don't you start her up and I'll see if I can figure it out."

Hank revved up the engine while Chafee leaned close to drown out the microphone he was wearing, and Agatha continued to write questions.

Does Tony have a gun?

Chafee shook his head and took the stylus from her.

Used to, he wrote.

Agatha took it back from him. *What happened to it?*

Hank revved the engine again.

Tony used to be a cop, but lasted less than a year. Gave the gun to Kip. Said he had no use for it.

Agatha bit at her bottom lip. That piece of information hadn't come up in any of their research. That would explain how he'd have access to police issued handcuffs.

Do you know where the pistol is?

In command center. Locked in bench.

What kind of weapon is it?

.45

Agatha snuck a look at Hank and nodded at him. He revved the engine again for good measure.

Can you bring it to us?

Maybe. Why?

She looked at Hank and he got out of the car to meet them under the hood. It was a gamble to trust Chafee, but there was no love lost between him and Tony. With Tony gone, Chafee's life would become a whole lot easier.

Possible murder weapon, she wrote.

Chafee's eyes got big and he stared at them a few seconds, trying to make a decision. He finally nodded, and Agatha let out a breath of relief, patting him on the shoulder.

Hank killed the engine and closed the hood.

"Well, Chafee, I'm not sure what you did, but it sure sounds better," Hank said. "Once again the Rio Chino Fire Department goes above and beyond."

"We're here to serve."

He waved as he mounted his oversized Fire Marshal's truck. Agatha and Hank waited as Chafee drove off, and they continued to keep watch for other cars, but there were none.

"Poor guy," Agatha said. "Stuck between a rock and a hard place."

"Yeah, I guess Tony is onto us. I figured we might have a little more time, but word spreads fast, and we've been talking to a lot of key people. Our biggest worry is that the gun will go missing."

"What do we do next?"

"Well, Aggie, I think our best bet is to reach out to the former police chief."

"Please stop calling me that." She pushed him playfully, but Hank wasn't expecting it and stumbled a few steps backward.

Bang.

A shot rang out and the glass in Hank's driver's side window exploded. Hank drew his weapon, and shoved Agatha down and dragging her as they bolted for cover behind his car.

"Aggie. Aggie, are you okay?" He asked her.

Agatha's heart was trying to jump out of her chest, and it had been a long time since she'd felt that kind of fear. "I'm okay."

Hank moved quickly to open the rear door on the passenger's side for more cover.

"Get in and lay on the floor."

She did as he said and stayed low to disappear into the back seat.

"I'm coming through," he said. "Stay clear."

In a flash, he dove in through the back door, and shimmied between the console and into the driver's seat.

"Keep your head down," he ordered.

Hank revved the engine and it roared like the beast it was designed to be. He stomped on the accelerator and the BMW launched out onto the road, and Hank ducked as he anticipated more gunfire. He peeked over the dash to see where the shooting was coming from, and he noticed a plume of dust in the distance. It wasn't a car. It was someone on a horse. A dang cowboy.

"Call Reggie Coil," he said to the voice controlled system in the car.

"Hank," Coil said. "I was about to call you."

"We need help." Hank shouted.

"What's wrong?"

"We're five miles south of Rio Chino. We just met with Peter Chafee, and he was wired for sound. Tony used to be a cop in the old days and he carried a .45. Same caliber as Julie's murder weapon. Tony's pistol is locked in the fire station. A couple of minutes after Chafee left a rifle round missed my head by less than a foot."

"What?" Coil asked. "Hang tight. I'm on my way."

"We're in the clear unless that cowboy chases us down at over one hundred miles an hour."

"Cowboy?"

"The shooter's on a horse."

"I'm on the police radio with a Texas Ranger. He's about fifteen miles from your location. Can you wait for him?"

"No," Agatha said from the back seat.

"It's not safe to stay put. We've got to get that gun." Hank cut in.

"I'm out of options, Hank. The combo of mayor, fire chief, and prosecutor have that town on lockdown. There's no way I can get those handcuffs or the pistol."

"Then call Walker, Texas Ranger," Agatha said as she climbed to the front seat. "There's gotta be something we can do."

"I've got an idea," Hank said.

"What are you up to, Hank?" Coil asked.

"Radio your Ranger friend and give him the description of my sedan. Tell him I'm heading to the fire station. Tell him I'm the shooter and still armed and dangerous."

"What?" Agatha said, her eyes widening. "Are you nuts?"

"What?" Coil yelled.

"Listen, if a search warrant can't get us in that fire station, maybe a high-speed chase will." Hank looked in his rearview mirror for the flashing lights.

"No way," Coil said. "That's suicide."

"If this car is as safe as advertised, then we'll be okay. Mostly. Once I crash through the sally port door, Aggie can jump out and make a run for the command post to get the pistol. The Ranger can arrest us and take the gun into custody. Then we can match ballistics and the case is solved."

"I'm not getting arrested or killed over this," Agatha said. "Unless you think the arrest will help with my research. Wait, this is nuts. Forget I said that. Have you been drinking?"

"I'm not going to sick a Texas Ranger on you," Coil said

"He shot at us. What am I supposed to do?" Hank asked furiously.

"You're not supposed to act like a rookie. This isn't Philadelphia, and you don't get what you want because you're Hammerin' Hank Davidson. This is like the wild west, son. The rules are different here."

Hank ended the call and slammed his fist on the dash.

CHAPTER FOURTEEN

"Hank, I know you're mad," Agatha said, trying to sound like she was completely calm. "But this isn't going to help anyone. Don't do this to us."

"If you hadn't pushed me out of the way, I'd be dead right now," he said.

"Believe me, I know. But being reckless will accomplish nothing."

"Is that what you think I am, too?" he asked. "Nothing?"

There was a desperation in his voice, and she realized this had more to do with him and his retirement than it had to do with his harebrained idea. She read people quickly and easily. It was part of her job. But Hank had done a good job of keeping the mask of control on all these months.

For the first time she truly saw his vulnerability. He wasn't only not good at being retired, he hated it. His entire identity had been that of a cop, and now that it was gone he felt like he was nothing.

"Hank, you were a great cop, but that's not all you are. You're a great man too. And the cop you were doesn't define the man you are now."

Agatha felt the car decelerate. She knew he was reconsidering.

"I'm no good away from the job," he said. "It's all I've ever known. I thought doing these investigations with you would help ease the slide into retirement."

"I think it has," she said. "But that doesn't mean there won't be bumps in the road."

"I was fine until that guy shot at us. I've got to be able to protect you. I hate feeling helpless."

"Helpless?" You're anything but helpless."

Sirens blared from behind them and Hank pulled off to the side of the road. Agatha let out a breath of relief that he'd reconsidered his insane idea.

"Just so you know," she said. "Chafee just texted. He got the pistol and hid it in the men's bathroom. He said he felt he needed to act fast, so he stashed it."

"Perfect."

"Driver, step out of the car with your hands in the air," said the voice over the loud speaker.

"I guess Coil changed his mind about helping me," Hank said, grinning.

Hank exited the sedan with his hands raised and quickly headed to the rear of his car to meet the Ranger. Agatha watched them chat for a bit before he called her to join them, and she breathed a sigh of relief that he wasn't in trouble

"Aggie, this is William Ellis. He's a Texas Ranger."

"Howdy, ma'am." Will tipped his Stetson with the Texas star mounted on the front.

The man was at least three inches taller than Hank's six-feet-two inches. He was rail thin and his features were hawkish. But his dark brown eyes were all cop.

"Thanks for not arresting Hank," she said.

He grinned. "Coil explained the situation. I'm in the area on order of the governor himself. My marching orders are to do whatever it takes to clear this mess up. Looks like working with y'all is the best way to get that done."

"Nick came through," she said to Hank.

"Money works in mysterious ways," Hank said. "We appreciate your help."

"Can you get me up to speed?"

Agatha listened as Hank ran down all the details from top to bottom.

"We think we've found the gun Tony used to kill Julie," Hank said. "We also discovered that even though the hand-cuffs attached to Julie were police issue, McCoy still had his on the duty belt. There's a receipt and description of it. Fletcher used to be a cop, so the probability is high they're his. The coroner, Dr. Anna Rusk has been helpful. The police chief might be helpful too, but I think he's under the mayor's thumb."

"Is the mayor involved?" Will asked.

"We've not heard that he was," Agatha said. "But it seems like everyone pretty much does Tony's bidding. He's got a lot of power and influence."

"We've got the fire marshal working on the inside for us," Hank said. "He's the one who alerted us about the possible murder weapon, and he's hidden it for us in the fire station bathroom so we can run ballistics."

"Chafee?" Will asked. "I know him. He's kinda hard to read at times, but I think he has a good heart."

"We've got nothing left to do but wait for Chafee to get that gun out after hours and get it to us. Why don't we meet back at the coroner's office at nine o'clock and see if he shows up with it? Then you can take it for ballistics."

"Sounds good. I know if the state crime lab ran analysis on the projectile, there will be a record for comparison."

Agatha was relieved. She'd get to make it back home for her dinner with Heather after all.

CHAPTER FIFTEEN

Thursday

Hank handed Agatha a to-go cup of hot tea as he climbed into her Jeep the next morning. He was relaxed and refreshed. He could feel things coming to a head. They'd have the real murderer behind bars before too much longer.

"I'm still furious about that gun shot." Hank greeted her.

"Me too. Let's keep our eyes open and heads low," She pretended to duck bullets.

"Deal." He smiled behind dark shades.

"Lord, I've been up for hours," she said, taking the tea. "I couldn't get my mind to shut off after Chafee texted last night and said he'd put the gun in the dumpster behind the Chinese restaurant. I'm ready to meet Ranger Will and get this thing going. Maybe we can get him to retrieve the gun so we don't have to experience that smell again."

"Ranger Will?" Hank asked.

"He reminds me of Howdy Doody, or like he should be hosting a kids' TV show." She mused.

"He's an expert marksman and has commendations out

the wazoo. I wouldn't make it a point of getting on his bad side."

"I never get on anyone's bad side," she said. "I'm adorable."

"Debatable," Hank said. "Stop looking at your tea like that and pay attention to the road. I've never met anyone who has a tea obsession like you."

"It's life's elixir. I'm pretty sure I'd die without it. Or at least be really cranky all the time. I've texted Chafee twice this morning, but he hasn't replied. Should we be worried?"

"It's eight o'clock in the morning. Why would we be worried?"

"Intuition. I think he's maybe gotten in over his head trying to play both sides of the field. We're the good guys and we know what he's doing with eyes wide open. We understand he's got to protect himself. But Tony's going to do whatever it takes to cover his own rear."

"We'll give him a chance to keep doing the right thing until he doesn't. So far he's come through for us."

"You're right," she said. "There's something different about you this morning. You've got a glow about you."

"I can feel it coming to an end."

"I think you're excited to see Dr. Rusk. Maybe you should give her one of those notes with the check boxes so she can mark yes or no if she likes you."

"Shut up and drive, Aggie."

"Grumpy. It must be love."

THEY PULLED into the rear parking lot of the Chinese restaurant, and the dumpster was piled extra high. There was a swarm of flies, and Hank felt his gorge rise at the thought of wading into the mess. He'd rather deal with a hundred bodies than go dumpster diving.

It was almost nine o'clock, and there was still no word from Chafee. He was starting to worry.

"Maybe he skipped town," Agatha suggested.

"He's the fire marshal. Where's he going to go?"

Agatha shrugged.

"We might as well get out and start looking," Hank said. "Can't chance the garbage truck won't pass today. Goodness knows it needs to. We used to have rookies do this stuff for us."

"Looks like you're the rookie now. I'll apologize ahead of time if I throw up on you."

"You can wait in the Jeep if you want," he said.

"No, we're partners. As much as I want to take you up on that offer, I'm going to suffer through it with you."

Hank dug around in his bag and handed Agatha a bandana. "Tie it over your face. Maybe it'll help with the smell some."

They got out of the Jeep and started combing the area. It was like looking for a needle in a haystack. As the sun came out and the morning faded, the heat made the smell worse. If that was possible.

"It's not out here," Hank said, wiping the sweat off his brow. He chugged water from one of the bottles stocked in the Jeep.

"You think this was a set up?" Agatha asked.

"I don't know. My instincts say he was being tested, but he's legitimate in his profile. I'm worried like you are."

Hank decided to text Coil.

No gun found. Think it was a setup.

Coil texted back.

Turn on your news. It's everywhere. Chafee dead. Be careful.

Hank called Agatha over and showed her the text messages.

"Ohmigosh," Agatha said. "Someone must have followed him after he hid the gun and taken it. Then they tracked him down and killed him."

Hank let out a flurry curses. "Let's get over to the coroner's office. Maybe Will can get a K9 team out here to look for the gun, just in case we missed it."

He crumpled the empty bottle in his fist and threw it at the cluttered dumpster, but it fell out onto the ground.

"You missed," she teased.

"Not today, Aggie."

"But you never miss, or at least that's what you claim."

"I tossed that stick of gum in your mouth from across the room didn't I?" Hank defended himself.

"In all fairness, I moved my head."

"Whatever. I bet you I can put that bottle in that gap right there." Hank pointed at the side of the dumpster.

"You're on, sassy pants."

He sighed and went over to the water bottle to pick it up. When he bent over something caught his eye.

"Well, well," he said. "Lookie here. Chafee came through after all." He knelt in a puddle of something, but it didn't matter. He reached between the dumpster and an old bicycle rack. The handle of the Colt .45 caliber, model 1911 pistol was barely visible as it had been concealed by the wrappings of a vape-cigarette package.

"Give me your bandana," he said.

Hank used it to pick up the .45.

"Thank God," she said. "Poor Chafee."

"He died a hero," Hank said. When he stood back up he held the .45 in one hand and the water bottle in the other.

"Umm..." Agatha said. "What's going on with that bottle?"

Hank beamed in a coat of sweat and a ray of pride.

"A bet's a bet, Aggie."

She scoffed, "We got more important things to do, Hank."

Hank hurled the water bottle over his head in a classic hook shot. A trickle of the water that had remained in the bottle sprinkled in an arc as the bottle lofted across his head and sailed through the morning's mist of back alley mosquitos and funk. Neither spoke as he sucked in a slight huff of air. The bottle spun slowly across the divide. It landed softly, soundly and certainly into the small gap Hank had identified.

"Bam. Now pay up, baby."

"Baby?" Agatha sneered. "Nice shot, let's go."

"Yeah, thanks." Hank chuckled as he withdrew his weapon from the holster.

Agatha ducked behind the Jeep.

"What's going on?" she whispered.

"Just being very cautious. Someone wants this gun back really bad. Bad enough to kill for it." He spoke quietly. "We need to get over to meet Will right now. Don't let anyone stop you from driving that Jeep right to her front door. Even if you have to drive through them. Can you do that?"

"I can do anything if it means taking that jerk Tony down," Agatha said.

IT WAS close to ten when Agatha skidded into the coroner's

back parking lot. He'd called Will ahead of time and let him know they were on the way. Will was waiting for them, providing protection for the area.

"Sorry it took us so long," Hank said, once they were safely inside. "We almost gave up on finding it."

"No worries," Will said. "Anna and I got to know each other a little better. Sorry to hear about Chafee."

"Us too," Hank said.

"His body should've come here," Rusk said, "But they opted to have the medical examiner in Dallas do the job. They don't want me anywhere near it. They know I helped y'all."

"At least we've got the pistol," Hank said.

"I'm waiting to hear from the ATF to see if this weapon has any history. The serial number will allow them to know who bought it, and if it was sold." Will said.

"Yeah, once they use acid to get down to the stamped serial number. This one has been obliterated." Hank handed it to Will.

"And the plot thins," whistled Agatha.

"WE'VE STILL GOT to get those handcuffs," Rusk said.

"That's where I run out of ideas," Will exhaled.

"Don't you think if this weapon is registered to Tony, and was what he used in the police academy and during his short term with the police department, that we could get a subpoena for the handcuffs?" Hank asked.

"You're talking about post-conviction relief and not an active criminal investigation, Hank," Agatha said.

"Officially," Will said, "They've already convicted the guilty person. The fact that he pled guilty doesn't help our case either, but it's only active because we're looking at it.

And because Nick Dewey pulled enough strings to have the governor assign me to you."

"I'm not going to stop until we get a confession from Tony," Hank said.

"I wouldn't expect you to. I'd better get going," Will said. "We need proof of ballistics to back up the serial number if it comes back as a match. I'm heading to the State's regional lab to test fire this thing."

"Will?" Agatha called out.

He glanced back over his shoulder. "Yes, ma'am?"

"Be careful. They've killed twice already."

CHAPTER SIXTEEN

BETH, DR. RUSK'S YOUNG RECEPTIONIST SAT BUNDLED in a blanket at her desk. Hank could see her shivering beneath the covers.

"Is there nothing that can be done about the cold?" Hank asked.

"Turnover is high in this job because of it," she said. "But I'm tough. Dr. Rusk said the place is old, but until they insulate the building the way they should and give her proper autopsy rooms, we have to keep it this cold to maintain the integrity of the bodies."

"You're a trooper," he said.

"I guess it evens out," she said. "My second job is in an old warehouse attic area. It can get hot as heck. Fortunately, I just run in and out of there cataloguing stuff, so I don't have to stay too long in the heat. I'm surprised I'm not sick all the time."

"What kind of stuff do you catalogue?"

"Evidence," Beth chirped.

Hank's gut twisted. "Evidence? What kind of evidence is there to sort out?"

"You know. Crimes and stuff. I catalogue the evidence. A lot of it is junk, but the sergeant says we gotta hold onto it in case somebody claims it or the prosecutor wants it for trial. It's really a bunch of clutter that they keep piling in there. They pay me to go in and organize it all."

"Does Dr. Rusk know about this?" Hank asked.

Beth shrugged. "I told her I had a second job. I work three evenings a week and on Saturday mornings. She never asked what it was. You think she'll be mad?"

"No. I commend you for the hard work."

"The heat isn't nearly as bad as the rats," she volunteered.

"Rats? Don't they have it locked up tight?"

Hank felt a twinge of guilt for walking this innocent girl down a path of revealing the city's secrets, but if she knew about it, then others knew about it.

"They said once the budget allows for more money, they'll fix it up. But for now it's not really what I'd call a secure facility. Some of those holes are big enough for a whole army of rats to get through. The sergeant says it's mostly piles of junk nobody needs anymore."

"When do you go back to work there?"

"Normally I'd go in tonight, but with the game tomorrow, I'm off until Monday."

"Who else works out there?"

She laughed lightly.

"No one, silly. It's just an old abandoned warehouse. It's too hot for all day staffing."

"I've enjoyed our talk," Hank said. "They're probably wondering where I am."

He told her goodbye and used the temporary badge Anna had given him to get back to the secured area. Rusk and Agatha were inside pouring over the files again.

"Glad you're back," Agatha said. "Look at this." She shoved the photo of the handcuffs at him that they'd looked at the day before, but she handed him a magnifying glass.

"I noticed what looked like etchings, or serial numbers on the handcuffs. Is that what they are? Any chance of that number coming back to a person?" she asked.

"Aggie, that's brilliant. Those were not Smith and Wesson cuffs. They were the Peerless brand. The serial numbers are lot-batch numbers. We could trace them to where they were distributed. For example, if the Rio Chino PD purchased in bulk, they'd be listed on the lot-batch. We can send the number to an old friend of mine who works for Peerless," Hank said. "They're based in Springfield, Massachusetts. I'm sure it's just a quick database search."

Hank swallowed hard and knew what he was about to propose could affect friendships. "Do either of you believe that there is an area of gray within the law?" he asked.

"I think there's room for discretion," Rusk said, "But never a place for corruption."

"Agreed." Agatha said.

"How far can you bend the law before breaking it?" He asked.

"It would depend on your perception of the law. A child, for example, doesn't know it and cannot be expected to strictly adhere to it." Rusk said.

"I'm not talking about children," he said.

"I'm not either, but I'm giving you the benefit of the doubt." Rusk glared at him.

Hank saw that Agatha wanted nothing to do with the debate. He understood that what he'd do. He'd do alone. He was okay with that. The sense of liberation to work as far to one side of the spirit of the law as he chose as a civilian was an overpowering moment. While he wasn't adverse to bending the law that he'd served, he'd never break it.

"I've got something to do. How about I meet y'all back here later?"

"Hank," Agatha said. "What are you getting yourself into?"

"The right thing. Trust me. I'll be back soon."

CHAPTER SEVENTEEN

"TURN HERE," HANK SAID.

"Where are we going?"

"We're about to take a walk," Hank said.

Agatha didn't look convinced.

"Trust me," Hank said. "Just a walk."

His phone buzzed and he looked at the number. It was Nick Dewey.

"Nick, how fast can that fancy bird get you to San Antonio? I got a message from Sheriff Coil that he spoke with the police chief who got fired for asking too many questions about Julie's murder. He has a boat load of files and backup records. I need everything on Tony's short career as a cop. And look for inventory and equipment assignment sheets."

Nick confirmed the task and then hung up.

Hank motioned for Agatha to ease off the old road that paralleled the railroad. Miller's Row had seen better days and made Hank glad they were in the Jeep. Rocks and branches snapped beneath the knobby tires. Trees covered what looked like an old path into the rear of what was the temporary police evidence warehouse. He'd gotten the address from Beth before they'd left.

"What are we doing here, Hank?" she stopped the Jeep and put it in park.

"Let me be very clear once again," he said. "This is what *I'm* doing. If you come along, it just means that I am doing something and you are walking where I am doing it. It's cleaner that way."

"Okay, where am I walking while you're doing whatever you're doing?"

"You'll see."

They began a stroll through the thicket of trees. Fall in Texas wasn't anything like where he was from. Most of the trees still had their leaves, and there was only the slightest hint that they might change colors.

"Up there to the right," Hank said.

"What is?" she asked. "Oh, never mind. I forgot I was only walking."

"That's the spirit," he said.

They came upon an old, two-story barn-like structure that looked long abandoned. There was a lock on the double front door, but a window on the second floor was missing.

"I really hope you're not bringing me out here to kill me," Agatha said.

"Rest that imagination of yours." He smiled.

"Thanks."

"Not this time." He made a crazy face.

"Oh, good," she said dryly. "You had me worried."

"This is where the police department stores their old evidence and recovered property. Most is probably junk, but I've gotta know if those cuffs are out here."

"I thought they'd be in the prosecutor's office." She commented.

"Do you know how much stuff is stored as evidence? Most cities could take up three or four super Wal-Marts with stuff. Vehicles, boats...you name it and cops stash it. The prosecutor isn't going to keep decades of stuff in their fancy office downtown."

"But would they really stick it out here?"

"You'd be surprised. It's been ten years."

He led her up a set of stairs that ran alongside the building. They shimmied around an old balcony and then swung a leg across a gap and into the open window. They both understood the consequences of falling or getting hurt. It would be the fire department's job to respond. They'd be screwed.

"Are we breaking and entering?" Agatha looked around once she was on a solid floor.

"Did you break anything to enter?"

"I guess it's all in the interpretation. Let's look and leave as fast as we can, okay? I'm a writer, not a burglar."

"Deal. I don't want to be here any longer than we have to. My allergies are about to start up."

"I'm going to start calling you bubble boy," Agatha said. "This is Texas. Everyone has allergies. Go and get a shot for them like a normal person."

"Now you tell me," he said.

"Where do we start?" She raised her hands.

"Evidence is usually categorized by year, then month, and finally by date. Let's start back here."

Hank made his way to the far, opposite corner of the cluttered upstairs loft. He didn't know how long they'd been looking when Agatha let out a gasp. She was holding a shoebox-sized plastic container with a faded strip of masking tape that had the date they were looking for labeled on it.

Hank took the box from her and opened it up. There were miscellaneous bits and pieces from different cases that had been handled that night. But he lifted a manila envelope and felt the chill of excitement pebble on his skin. The envelope was heavy, and he opened it and slid the contents onto a table. It was a pair of single chain handcuffs.

"I can't take them with us," he said. "It's just not ethical. But at least we know it's here."

"*You* can't take them with you," she said. "It's that cop in you. But I have no problem taking them with me."

Agatha used her shirt to keep from touching the cuffs and slid them back in the envelope. "Let's go. There's a good guy rotting in a state penitentiary for nothing. I'm not going to allow that to continue one day longer than it has too."

"I've never seen this side of you, Aggie."

"When it comes to helping the underdog, you better get used to it. I spent my youth afraid because the rules failed to protect me. No more, Hammering Hank."

Once they returned to the Jeep, she handed him the keys.

"I'm too jacked up to drive," she said. "I don't think I'm cut out for a life of crime."

"Jacked up on what, Aggie?"

"Justice."

The two crept back out the way they arrived and headed toward Rusk's office.

They called Rusk, who opened the rear door for them. They also saw the Texas Ranger's vehicle and hoped it was Will.

"Hey, guys," Will said.

"We were just saying how we hoped it was you," Agatha said. "I can't take any more surprises today."

"That's a switch. Most people don't like me being around at all." He held out an envelope. "I thought I'd give you this in person."

Agatha peeled open the envelope and breathed a sigh of relief.

"The ballistics match," she told Hank.

"And ATF confirmed that Tony purchased the weapon at a gun show in Houston the month before he entered the police academy. And, not surprisingly, TCOLE has two years of records with him shooting a qualifying score with that same pistol."

"We've got a murder weapon," Hank said. "But we can't prove it was Tony who pulled the trigger. We've got to put Tony in that house with Julie."

"Well, we're back to being screwed then without those handcuffs." Will grumbled.

"Oh, what's this?" Rush asked, noticing the evidence envelope Agatha had snuck onto her desk. She read the writing on the envelope. "October twenty-nine two thousand and eight." Then she looked up at them. "What did y'all do?"

"I just walked," Agatha said.

Hank rolled his eyes. "You don't think one of those honest police detectives planted that in here to help solve the case, do you?" Hank asked, leading her to her answer.

"Open it," Agatha begged.

"If this is what I think it is, we've got to return it," Rusk said.

"If that's what I'm sure it is," Will said, playing along, "And one of those brave cops took the chance to bring it here, then there is no way I'm going to disrespect them and also put their lives in jeopardy by making city officials aware they left it." Will reached over and ripped the envelope open.

Hank suddenly felt less horrible about initiating everything. Will was right. Brave people put themselves at risk to help an ex-cop who did nothing more than play high school football, get free.

"It's a match," Agatha said, comparing the cuffs to the crime scene photograph."

"What now?" Rusk asked.

"Will, can your people at the lab process these cuffs?" Hank asked. "There may be a latent or partial print. Tony's would be perfect, but anything would help."

"Well, looks like I'm back off to the regional crime lab. It'll take a bit to process and then search matches. How about we all head out of here and let the good doctor get back to her work."

They all headed for the door, and Hank turned back to Anna. "You going to be okay here alone?" Hank asked.

"I'm fine. No one is going to mess with me. And if they try, I know how to defend myself." She held up her fists in a fighting stance. "I'm a Philly girl, remember?"

He hoped she was right.

CHAPTER EIGHTEEN

FRIDAY

"Y'all two have been mighty scarce," Coil said. "Thought maybe you'd decided to elope."

It was the final Friday in October, and that meant cool weather and hot football rivalries. Rusty Gun had her own 1-A team, and it was the pride of the town.

"So where do y'all stand right now?" Coil asked.

"We have the .45 and ballistics to show it's a match for the weapon that killed Julie McCoy. We have ATF records showing Tony bought that same gun, and Texas State records showing he attended the police academy and qualified with that same gun."

"That's pretty darn good," Coil said.

Agatha added. "Unfortunately, we have a weapon transfer form showing Tony gave the pistol to Kip Grogan right after he joined the fire service. And Kip kept it under his control in his command center."

"That's not so good," Coil said.

"But, we also have the handcuffs used to lock Julie to the bed while her home was burning. And we have the 911 recording that has Tony and Kip talking about the pistol. So, Tony did know where it was and had access too," Hank explained.

Coil stared at them with his mouth open. "You have that handcuffs?"

"Yep," Agatha replied.

"How?" Coil leaned forward. "Do I want to know?"

"We think one of the detectives working the Chafee case left it at the coroner's office for us to discover," Hank said.

"Uh huh," Coil said, clearly reading between the lines. "What else do you need?"

"We need to place Tony in the house with Julie. Will is processing the handcuffs for prints, and I'm running down records on those cuffs to show ownership or assignment."

"You guys are close," Coil said. "It's a heck of a job. But be careful. Tony is going to be desperate, and people get a little crazy around big game nights."

"I've noticed," Hank said.

"Still no lead on who shot at you?" Coil asked.

"Not yet, but I'm going to bet ballistics shows it's the same rifle that killed Chafee."

HANK AND AGATHA motored back toward Rio Chino for the sixth day in a row. The drive was a good time to brief and discuss investigative tactics, but they were quiet this morning. It had been a long week and they were both physically and emotionally spent. Agatha kept the Jeep at a comfortable speed while Hank fielded a call from Will.

When he hung up he asked, "You know where Salado is?"

"Sure. What's wrong?"

"We're meeting Will there."

"Why?"

"They found a print. It matches a guy by the name of Benjamin Guise. He was arrested by Tony for loitering in October 2010. Will ran an arrest records audit and guess what? Tony made one single arrest in his entire career as a cop. Can you imagine? What a wuss. Anyway, that honor goes to Benjamin Guise of Salado, Texas."

"Wow," she said.

"Wow, indeed. We're nailing his coffin shut a little at a time."

When they got to Salado she pulled the Jeep next to Will's car in the official police parking lot.

"Great timing," Will said.

"She's a speeder."

"We still wouldn't be here if Hank was driving," she teased with Will.

"Then in that case, I'm glad you were driving. Y'all come on in."

They got out of the car and followed Will into the municipal building. He led them into a small interview room. They were introduced to a nice looking man in an automotive shop uniform. His name tag read Ben. Will asked Ben to recount his arrest story.

He confirmed it that while he waited outside for friends, that Tony walked up in his police uniform and began harassing him. Ben said Tony was with a woman.

"Is this the woman?" Ben asked, showing him a picture.

"Oh, yeah. That's her," he said, nodding. "You don't forget a face like hers. The most beautiful woman I've ever seen. He was showing off for her big time. That's the only reason he arrested me."

Tony's prints had also been on the handcuffs, but cops swapping cuffs wasn't uncommon. But Ben's one time arrest and Tony's only ever arrest just sealed the deal. It was confrontation time.

Agatha and Hank agreed to meet Will back at Rusk's office. Will would need the help of the Texas State Attorney General, Ava Grace O'Brien to make the arrest on a town's fire chief. Especially since there was a man already convicted of the crime. It was going to be a major headache of paperwork and politics for Will, but they knew he didn't mind one bit. As long as justice was served.

Hank called Nick Dewey and let him know what they'd discovered, but warned him against telling Gage or his grandson anything. Nothing was certain, and that was for sure.

They got in the car and headed back to Rio Chino.

"Ohmigosh," she said when they entered town. "Where are we?"

"I think it's Rio Chino, but I can't be sure," Hank said in disbelief. "I've never seen a town this decorated. It's like *Party City* threw up."

The small town was completely covered in yellow and red, and anything that had a tiger image. The Pumpkin Bowl was just hours away, and they could sense the adrenaline pulsating in the atmosphere. Coil was right, things were different on game night.

Will's unit already sat in the rear parking lot of the coroner's office. Hank ran his knuckles across the top of the hood like Agatha had seen him do often. Will's car was still warm. Rusk shoved the door open. Her scowl spoke volumes. Agatha noticed a chair knocked over.

"What's going on?" she asked, but was afraid to know.

She saw Will display an outburst that needed no explanation. It was politics at its worst.

"Talk to me, Will," Hank said.

"State's AG says they would consider moving to drop the conviction on Gage, but they didn't feel there was enough evidence to charge Tony. They said politically, everyone should be able to swallow at least one man being set free with no admission of prosecutorial errors from the State on McCoy's conviction."

"What?" Agatha asked.

"Tony remains untouchable," Rusk said.

"Well, at least Gage goes free and his son gets his dad back. Right?" Hank said, but Agatha didn't believe for one second that Hank was satisfied with the decision.

"Sometimes you have to take what you can get," Will said, the disappointment evident in his voice. "If it's all the same to you folks, I've got about a month of reports to write up on this. I'm heading back to HQ, and will catch up with y'all Monday."

"Thanks, Will," Agatha said as she hugged him.

Hank shook his hand and then watched Rusk escort him out.

"What do we do now?" Agatha asked. She picked up the knocked over chair and collapsed into it.

Hank didn't answer her, but he called Nick and gave him the latest update. As expected, the man was overwhelmed. His grandson's father would soon be freed, yet his daughter's killer would remain free. He was furious. And he had every right to be.

"I'm ready to get out of here," Agatha said. It was obvious her mood had turned sour fast.

"Umm, have you seen the streets? We're not going anywhere. There's a parade of cars and buses farther than you can see. We might as well head on over to see what's so great about the Iron Pumpkin game."

"You coming, Doc?" Agatha asked.

"Not in a million years," she said. "I hate this day with a passion. It's the same every year. Hopefully this will be my last year here."

Hank and Agatha waved goodbye and walked to the stadium. There were tailgating parties going on in the parking lot, and the crowd was unbelievable. They bought tickets and slipped through the horde, grabbing a low corner bench not far from where the fire department and ambulance set up operations. And there in all of his glory was Rio Chino Fire Chief Tony Fletcher.

"Better get that look off your face," Hank said. "He's bound to notice you want to kill him."

"You did tell me never to play poker," she said, looking away from Tony. "Oh look, here comes the band." Agatha sat up with a little excitement along with more people filing into the stadium.

"Ladies and gentlemen," a voice came across the loud speaker. "I'm Principle E.G. Sharp, and I'm with your favorite head football coach, MT "Tic" Tatum."

The crowd went nuts. The man was a legend.

"We're here to honor the greatest football team that ever played at Rio Chino High School. They're still known simply as, "The Team.""

Applause exploded as the band whipped them up into a frenzy.

"I want to honor The Team by bringing the surviving players out to join me, and to honor those who have passed."

"Now this is what high school football should be about," Agatha said. "Respect."

She scooted closer to Hank as the brisk night air cooled

things off considerably. They listened to the names and the cheers as they assumed family members and grandfathers were being honored.

"Offensive tackle Blake Smith. Offensive Guard Wilber Martin. Quarterback Emory Harley. Fullback Velton Flowers."

"Did he just say Emory Harley?" Agatha asked, feeling the bottom fall out of her stomach.

"Yes."

"That's my dad. I had no idea. My mom grew up in Rusty Gun, but my dad never talked about where he was from. He'd had a bad childhood, so it was just kind of understood that we didn't ask him about it."

Agatha burst into tears and Hank put his arm around her, pulling her close.

"Sorry," she said, wiping her face. "I'm not usually this emotional. I think I'm ready to go home."

They walked quietly back to her Jeep. Hank opened the passenger side door for her, and he drove. She needed the space. Hank eased around poor parking, RV campers and BBQ bits still lit before he finally found the exit. He stopped suddenly at the wail of sirens. Looking to his left he saw the same fire truck parked at the game following behind Tony in his bright colored chief's truck.

"You curios?" Hank asked.

"I'll admit that I am," she said.

Hank turned right instead of back to the left and home to Rusty Gun. It wasn't quite seven o'clock yet, so they had time. The pulsing scream of the engine was easy to follow, and when they clipped about two miles outside of town, he saw what they were responding to. It was a giant ball of fire. It looked like a barn or something like it.

Hank turned off his headlights and eased up probably

closer than he should have. It wasn't a barn. Agatha looked to say something and saw Hank's mouth fall open as his expression blanked into horror.

"Oh, no," Hank said. "That's Nick's helicopter."

"You sure?" Agatha questioned. "How do you know it's his?"

"Positive. You can still see the logo on the side."

The multimillion dollar state of the art private chopper sat in the middle of a cow pasture in flames.

"This is my fault. I shouldn't have told him about Tony getting away with killing Julie. He was probably so upset he lost control."

"Speaking of Tony," Agatha said. "There he goes."

The hairs on the nape of his neck stood up and he searched the landscape, looking for what had caused it. "Look," he said, pointing off to the right. He started to open the car door, helpless to do anything.

Agatha looked to the right of the burning heap. The violent and vicious fingers of reddish orange flames clawed through the helicopter's wreckage and licked into the cool of an ink black night. But the flames exposed a shadow.

It was Nick. It had to be. And he was squatted on one knee, his hunting rifle raised. He fired one shot while Hank and Agatha watched helplessly. Tony dropped to the ground where he stood.

Agatha didn't flinch, and Hank didn't hold her. There was nothing to say. Hank shifted the Jeep into reverse, and drove through the empty field until they were back on the roadway. He turned left and headed for Rusty Gun.

"There are all kinds of justice," Agatha finally said.

Hank rested his hand on her arm.

"Isn't that the truth."

SNEAK PEEK: BOOK 3

Download Now - I Saw Mommy Killing Santa Claus

December 24, 2004

"But I'm not sleepy." Ellie yawned and rubbed her eyes, and her daddy nuzzled against the top of her head. She loved when he did that.

"Honey, you know Santa Claus is waiting to bring your toys," he said. "But you have to go to sleep first."

She was too excited to sleep. Santa was coming. And she was going to catch him this year.

"Ellie," her mother said. "Let's get your teeth brushed and then you can set out the cookies and milk for Santa."

"Can we feed the reindeer too?" she asked. "Rudolph is my favorite. The others were so mean to him. But he showed them. He got revenge by leading the pack. He deserves a special snack."

"Ellie Bear," her daddy said. "The point of the story isn't revenge. Rudolph was just different, and it took an effort to see that being different didn't mean bad. He had special blessings, and it just took his friends awhile to see that."

Daddy had that worried look in his eyes he got sometimes when she said something she shouldn't. But she didn't see anything wrong with what she'd said.

"When I was being different, the doctor said I was being bad," Ellie said, her bottom lip quivering.

"Honey, that's completely different. What you were doing to those animals was wrong. Very wrong. But you've stopped, and you're all better now."

Ellie snickered beneath her breath. Her daddy thought she'd stopped. She'd just learned to be sneakier. They just didn't understand why she did it.

"I did stop playing with animals like the doctor told me too," she lied. "I'm a good girl."

He sighed and the worried look didn't go away. "You sure are trying, honey bunch. But you've got to stop hurting the other children."

She kicked out with her feet, tired of the conversation. It was always about what she couldn't and shouldn't do. Nobody let her have any fun.

"But the kids aren't animals," she said. "They can run away if they don't like it. They're not helpless."

"Baby, you shouldn't hurt anybody or anything. I know you don't want to be a bad girl. You're so smart, and we love you very much."

She grinned and hugged his neck. "I love you, daddy."

"Enough stalling, little girl," her mom said. "Time for bed or no Santa."

Ellie narrowed her eyes at her mother and gave her an angry face, and she smiled when her mother backed up a step. She liked that she could scare them.

"Honey, mommy is just excited to get Santa's cookies

and milk set out so we can go to bed too. We're excited about Santa coming."

"Oh, daddy. You're too big for Santa," she said, giggling.

"Santa has something special for everyone. Even grownups."

Ellie got ready for bed, put out the cookies and milk, and then hopped into bed. Her mommy tucked her in nice and tight, just how she liked.

"I know Santa will love those special cookies," he mother said. "He might even share with Rudolph. Now be a good girl and go nighty-night. We'll see you in the morning."

Ellie snuggled under the covers, and despite her best intentions, was asleep in moments. But hours later she was stirred by a bump. Excitement filled her at the thought of Santa trying to get down their tiny chimney. She was going to catch him and keep him. There was no reason for the other kids to get all the toys.

She slid out of bed, the wood floor cold beneath her feet, and she frowned as she her the soft murmur of voices. It didn't sound like Santa Claus. She peered down the hall. The cramped living room was bathed by shimmering lights that cast a mystical glow. Her eyes were still foggy from the sleepy film of exhaustion, but she knew what she was seeing.

"Santa," she whispered, eyeing the man in the red suit with awe.

Her eight-year-old heart fluttered in her chest, and she stayed still against the wall as he put presents under the tree. And then she heard another voice, and took the chance of peeking around the corner for a better look.

"Mommy," she said, her voice soft. And then she gasped and put her hand over her mouth so they wouldn't hear her. Santa had hugged her mom and pulled her in for a kiss. A long kiss. Rage filled her from the tips of her toes to the top of her head, and she felt hot all over. Daddy was going to be so upset when she told him. So hurt. She had the best daddy in the world and he didn't deserve that.

"I hate Christmas," she said. "And Santa."

Ellie crept back to her bed, her face wet with angry tears. She jerked the quilted afghan up to her chin, but there'd be no going to sleep. Her heart was broken. Were mommy and daddy going to divorce like Ronny's parents had?

She tried to sleep, but the voices in her head wouldn't leave her alone. They were yelling at her, screaming at her to do something. She was the only one who could make things right.

Ellie wasn't sure how she got in the kitchen. She just opened her eyes and she was there. And then in a flash she was standing in her parent's bedroom, holding the lighter fluid and the matches, and the voices in her head were telling her what to do.

"I hate Christmas," she said. And then she poured the lighter fluid on and around their bed and lit the match.

She felt the whoosh of the fire as she turned around and went back to her room. Maybe now she could finally get some sleep.

Liliana and I have loved sharing these stories in our Harley & Davidson Mystery Series with you.

There are many more adventures to be had for Aggie and Hank. Make sure you stay up to date with life in Rusty Gun, Texas by signing up for our emails.

Thanks again and please be sure to leave a review where you bought each story and, recommend the series to your friends.

Kindly,
Scott & Liliana

Enjoy this book? You can make a big difference

Reviews are so important in helping us get the word out about Harley and Davidson Mystery Series. If you've enjoyed this adventure Liliana & I would be so grateful if you would take a few minutes to leave a review (it can be as short as you like) on the book's buy page.

Thanks,
Scott & Liliana

ALSO BY LILIANA HART

The MacKenzies of Montana

Dane's Return

Thomas's Vow

Riley's Sanctuary

Cooper's Promise

Grant's Christmas Wish

The MacKenzies Boxset

MacKenzie Security Series

Seduction and Sapphires

Shadows and Silk

Secrets and Satin

Sins and Scarlet Lace

Sizzle

Crave

Trouble Maker

Scorch

MacKenzie Security Omnibus 1

MacKenzie Security Omnibus 2

JJ Graves Mystery Series

Dirty Little Secrets

A Dirty Shame

Dirty Rotten Scoundrel

Gone to Dust

Say No More

Lawmen of Surrender (MacKenzies-1001 Dark Nights)

1001 Dark Nights: Captured in Surrender

1001 Dark Nights: The Promise of Surrender

Sweet Surrender

Dawn of Surrender

The MacKenzie World (read in any order)

Trouble Maker

Bullet Proof

Deep Trouble

Delta Rescue

Desire and Ice

Rush

Spies and Stilettos

Wicked Hot

Hot Witness

Avenged

Never Surrender

Stand Alone Titles

Breath of Fire

Kill Shot

Catch Me If You Can

All About Eve

Paradise Disguised

Island Home

The Witching Hour

ALSO BY LOUIS SCOTT

Books by Liliana Hart and Louis Scott

The Harley and Davidson Mystery Series

The Farmer's Slaughter

A Tisket a Casket

I Saw Mommy Killing Santa Claus

Get Your Murder Running

Deceased and Desist

Malice in Wonderland

Tequila Mockingbird

Gone With the Sin

American Police & Military Heroes series

Call Of Duty

FAST

Rapid Fire

End Of Watch

A DEA Undercover Thriller series

SAINT

JUSTICE

SINNER

Cajun Murder Mystery Short-Story Series

By The Numbers (#1)

The Shepherd (#2)

Geaux Tiger (#3)

Cajun Cooking (#4)

Crooked Cross (#5)

Cracked Cross (#6)

Double Cross (#7)

Creole Crossroads (#8)

Bayou Backslide: Special Novella Edition

Bayou Roux: The Complete First Season

F.O.R.C.E Adventure Series

The Darkest Hour

Split Second

New York Minute

Liliana Hart is a New York Times, USAToday, and Publisher's Weekly bestselling author of more than sixty titles. After starting her first novel her freshman year of college, she immediately became addicted to writing and knew she'd found what she was meant to do with her life. She has no idea why she majored in music.

Since publishing in June 2011, Liliana has sold more than six-million books. All three of her series have made multiple appearances on the New York Times list.

Liliana can almost always be found at her computer writing, hauling five kids to various activities, or spending time with her husband. She calls Texas home.

If you enjoyed reading *this*, I would appreciate it if you would help others enjoy this book, too.

Lend it. This e-book is lending-enabled, so please, share it with a friend.

Recommend it. Please help other readers find this book by recommending it to friends, readers' groups and discussion boards.

Review it. Please tell other readers why you liked this book by reviewing. If you do write a review, please send me an email at lilianahartauthor@gmail.com, or visit me at http://www.lilianahart.com.

Connect with me online:
www.lilianahart.com
lilianahartauthor@gmail.com

facebook.com/LilianaHart

twitter.com/Liliana_Hart

instagram.com/LilianaHart

bookbub.com/authors/liliana-hart

Liliana's writing partner and husband, Scott blends over 25 years of heart-stopping policing Special Operations experience.

From deep in the heart of south Louisiana's Cajun Country, his action-packed writing style is seasoned by the Mardi Gras, hurricanes and crawfish étouffée.

Don't let the easy Creole smile fool you. The author served most of a highly decorated career in SOG buying dope, banging down doors, and busting bad guys.

Bringing characters to life based on those amazing experiences, Scott writes it like he lived it.

Lock and Load – Let's Roll.

Made in the USA
San Bernardino, CA
20 March 2020

65989528R00093